Pelts

Phil Scott Mayes

~~Men~~ shout.
They curse. They profane.
Blood soaked hands
proclaim their virility.
Callous fools admire it.
Through rended flesh
and plundered souls,
they strive to *feel*
like men.

This story is for you, Azariah.
Laugh, cry, love.
Fight if you must.
Be your own man.
You will always be enough.

I love you, Son.

1

Magnus Lief wandered the dense, subalpine forest searching the firs and pinyons for the markings he had made five years earlier. He circled a massive ponderosa pine dragging his fingers over bark ridges so thick they could've been tree trunks themselves.

"I remember these trees quite differently," Magnus said. He scanned up the trunk until his head rested between his shoulder blades. Blue pinholes of afternoon sky winked through the dense canopy. "The growth is incredible; it's as thick as the Amazon!"

"Is it really?" Ingrid's tone was curious, but Magnus couldn't help doubting her sincerity.

More focused on the foliage than his words, he said, "I don't suppose you made it down that way, did you?"

"You know I traveled north."

"Yes, yes. I know." When the forest began to spin, he lowered his gaze to Ingrid. "I can't find our markings. Have we returned to the wrong mountain?"

Magnus regarded the woman he had known for several lifetimes. The bonnet didn't suit her, nor the dress, but he supposed his beige wool suit looked equally ridiculous. She appeared uncomfortable in her lily-white skin, gazing back through weary blue eyes. Subtle bags had formed beneath them, and her jawline bore the suggestion of jowls. Still, she looked young—certainly younger than him. His bags weren't subtle, his jowls fully formed, and unlike her bright yellow hair, his was mostly gray. But side by side the most obvious observation would be how her shapely figure stood four inches taller than his, which was *a* shape, that of a bulging sack of grain.

Ingrid attempted a smile. "This *has* to be the mountain, Magnus. Wrong isn't an option. We've led forty settlers out here on the promise of gold. They won't be happy when we don't deliver, but that doesn't matter as long as we make it to the crater."

Magnus walked to the next tree and searched for markings. "It's not their feelings that worry me. It's the pelts. We're almost out of time. You know this, Ingrid."

Ingrid sighed. "You worry too much. We'll have the pelts in a day's time."

"I suppose." Magnus chewed his lip. "I wouldn't worry so much if I could just find my markings. Tell me, dear Ingrid, have I shrunk?"

"By every dimension save your circumference." She winked, and a chortle climbed up Magnus' throat as Ingrid cackled. Then, all too soon, the lightheartedness ended.

Magnus scanned the trees and stole another glance at Ingrid. If their quest for pelts was successful, they would soon have everything they needed to raise an abundant family. She would make a splendid partner in that. He watched her eyes dance from trunk to trunk then bloom with excitement.

"Magnus," she cried, "isn't that one right there?"

He traced her sightline upward to find gouges in the tree at least forty feet from the ground. "It can't be. They can't have grown that much. I marked them at eye level with my hatchet—"

"Dear God, what *is* that?" The settler's fearful shout came from behind.

Magnus turned and found a woman gaping at something beyond him. He spun, sidestepped the tree, and saw a gargantuan shape standing not fifty feet away in a veil of shadows. His pulse drubbed in his ears as it ambled into the sun's golden rays.

It was almost a moose. Almost.

Its muscles were bulging boulders, its tines sharpened spears with splintered barbs. A horn grew through a crusted split in its snout, and along its spine were bony protrusions like the points of a wrought iron fence. From its hind quarters flicked long ropes of hair embedded with jagged shards of something, maybe bone.

A gunshot sent a jolt through Magnus' body. The blast resounded from tree to tree in all directions and fingers of terror wiggled inside of him. He stared at the beast, flinching as more shots rang out from the throng of settlers. A cloud of sulfurous smoke drifted by Magnus, swirled around the trees, dissipated. The beast was unaffected. It stood strong, lowering its head to charge.

"Run for your lives!" Magnus yelled.

The settlers scattered in all directions. Fathers and mothers snatched up their little ones who screamed and cried and clung for dear life. When Magnus saw that Ingrid was fleeing, he bolted, outpacing the settlers with children in their arms and even Ingrid in that confounded dress. He approached a large pile of sticks and hurdled it in stride.

"Make for the edge of the wood!" he yelled.

As he neared another pile of sticks, a warning fluttered within. There were dozens of the unnatural mounds littering the forest floor. They hadn't fallen from the trees like that. Magnus veered around it, checking his flanks as he went.

To the left, a burly man stepped in a rut and pitched forward, landing beside a mound. The sticks hinged upward like a trapdoor and a wagon wheel-sized spider lurched forth. It sunk fangs the size of sickles into him and dragged him below.

Magnus slowed, pirouetted. Everywhere settlers toppled and vanished beneath the forest floor. "Sticks! Avoid the sticks!"

Rumbling grew from behind. The moose. It bellowed over the settlers' screams. Magnus accelerated and weaved through the trees. He forsook the settlers. He forgot the mountain. He fretted each perilous step. He thought only of running, and pelts, and freakish creatures, and then again of running. Eventually, the forest quieted. Only then did he stop. Only then, gasping and turning and rife with guilt, did he think of Ingrid.

Magnus called out to her.

A response came in the form of rustling leaves and clacking teeth. Magnus backtracked toward the awful sound. He found the moose in the shadow of an evergreen.

Ingrid was impaled on its rack. A tine protruded from her mouth, others through her left ribs and lower abdomen, and more through her legs. Her eyes were dim and still, her white skin already ashen gray. The typical rosé of her lips was now a deep plum.

"I'm sorry," he whispered, a tear plotting a warm trail down his cheek. Then he turned and ran eastward alone.

2

"Is tha game olmost ovah?" the harlot asked Lefty, hollering over the din of the saloon. Her lips grazed the fine hairs on the rim of Lefty's ear, sending a trickle down his neck. "I wanna have some foon." She ran a finger along his scruffy jaw and stopped at his chin, trying to turn him for a kiss. He resisted, cringing at the way her oily flesh glided along his.

"Yeah, Cap'n, you should quit while you's ahead." Corporal Brown hiccupped and reached with greedy fingers toward Lefty's stack of chips that was larger than everyone else's combined.

"Why quit when I'm 'bout to win?" Lefty asked.

"You're gointa win with doze cards?" the harlot asked, snickering as she peered over Lefty's shoulder.

He drove an elbow into her ribs, snarling, "Damn you, Uma! Get off, ya scab!"

His opponents laughed, and he wondered which they found funnier: his misfortune or the way Uma staggered away aping his outburst. Not that the answer mattered. She had played her part flawlessly, and he would reward her properly—after a bath, of course. He had the fools now.

"Shit, sir. Can't believe I'm 'bout to say this, but I reckon ya shoulda listened to Brown." Lefty's lieutenant creased a wry grin and pushed his remaining chips to the center of the table. "All in."

"That so, Dingo?" Lefty asked. "You think I should quit?"

He slid his left hand down the side of the wooden chair until he felt the leather strap tied there. Tugging it, he said, "Come here, boy," and the words conjured the shuffling of bare feet. *Blind beast's got more sense than the rest of em combined*, Lefty thought. He glanced over his shoulder.

"Here, Stickman, eat this," Brown said, placing a dead fly into the hungry boy's hand. The boy popped the fly into his mouth without hesitation and Lefty's men snickered like school yard bullies.

Lefty shook his head as Stickman's chewing face slid into his peripheral. "Have a look at these here cards an' tell me if you think I should quit."

Stickman swallowed, furrowing his brow as he scanned the cards with his cloudy eyes.

"But, Cap'n, he cain't see—"

Lefty shushed Brown. "Let him concentrate."

"He don't speak English neither," Dingo noted.

Lefty's glare crept to Dingo. "You so sure?"

There was a tap on Lefty's shoulder. He turned and met the unnerving gaze of Stickman's white marbles. The Indian boy wagged his head, bald except for lines of black stubble the drunken barber had missed. It seemed an intelligent response, not a guess, but that was impossible. Stickman would've had to understand the request...and the rules of the game...and be able to *see* the cards.

Lefty nodded and patted his pet on the shoulder. "I

thought not. Good advise, boy. Now stand back. Ya smell like shit." The men laughed. "Maybe I'll let ya have a bath while I celebrate this victory with Uma. You can...*watch* if ya like." The men laughed even harder at this, although Brown's lips pursed in confusion.

The laughter dwindled and Dingo said, "So you ain't quittin?"

"Stickman says to play."

"Damn, I's hopin for an easy one."

Blood chugged hotly through Lefty's neck. "You fools ain't learned a damned thing from me all these years. *Ahead* don't mean shit, quittin ain't an option, and *easy* is for pussies!"

"Anyone can quit, Captain, even you," said Bull. His sausage-like pinky pushed the small round spectacles up his nose until they were snugged beneath his caveman brow. They looked like children's glasses. The bows struggled to reach around his massive bald gourd to his undersized ears, and the tiny lenses barely covered the whites of his eyes.

Brown swayed and hiccupped. "Yeah, an' ahead *do* mean shit." He put forth both hands and moved them as if shaping a clay bowl to emphasize Lefty's mountain of chips. The imbecile then raised his right pointer toward the ceiling. Dingo and Bull glanced up. The finger hovered nearer and nearer to Brown's face until his eyes crossed. And then, abruptly, it was one knuckle deep inside his right nostril. He rooted around and yanked it out with a gleeful look of discovery, though nothing was there. He placed the invisible treasure atop his meager pile of chips, waving his hand with a magician's flourish.

"Weird shit, Brown, even for you," Dingo remarked, shaking his head.

Brown aimed the unclean finger at Dingo. "No. No. I has a point."

"I doubt it." Bull chuckled and Lefty could feel the bouncing of his heavy shoulders through the floorboards.

"I'm sayin…" Brown trailed off and his eyelids descended until only slits of white remained. They snapped open again, wide with enthusiasm. "Ya cain't make a pig's tail whistle! Dammit, no. I mean…ya cain't make a pig's tail out of a whistle. Ya cain't make a whistle out of a pig's tail? Shit, who cares? Point is, it ain't possible, like catchin up to Lefty here cause he's so *ahead*."

Dingo's jaw went slack. "Tie me over a barrel and nibble me with hen's teeth." Cocking his head and turning to Bull, he said, "He *did* have a point, an' it almost made sense!"

"Brown, you might be *smarter* when you're drunk," said Bull.

The nincompoops were getting off track.

"No, he ain't." Lefty leaned forward and pointed at Brown's chips. "How 'bout the finger up your nose? What point does that make?"

Brown's lips widened and drooped in a melting smile. "Even if I could pull chips from my fuckin honker—an' I cain't—I'd still never catch ya. B'sides, ya cain't lose money if ya don't play." Philosopher Brown nodded with satisfaction.

"That'd be true, except that the game don't end just cause I stop playin. I ain't playin against myself. I'm playin against you fools," he said, spearing the goofy young soldier with a manicured finger then raking around the room, "an' all the other fools out there. Me against the whole goddamn world. If I stop, the world catches up. Ya follow?"

"Mmhmm, thas true," Brown slurred, nodding crookedly. "Uma will end up with all yer money. Mine too if'm lucky!" He winked at Uma who was sitting in a chair beside their table, her bare feet propped on a crusty brass spittoon. She spread her knees and fluffed the lap of her dress, flashing Brown a glimpse of her tinder box and a yellow grin. When he looked up, she blew him a kiss.

Colluding with Uma wasn't necessary for Lefty to defeat anyone at that table, except maybe Bull. Bull had actually finished primary school and was good with numbers and logic, which was more than could be said for anyone else in the company. Still, Lefty never hazarded a loss.

It must be a bloodbath.

His men had to stagger away reeling, licking their wounds, and wondering what dumbheaded impulse drove them to challenge him in the first place. His men belonged firmly underfoot, in every way, always. Lives depended on their unwavering loyalty, their unflinching obedience. A moment's dithering was the difference between claiming a sack of Indian scalps as good as a leprechaun's pot-o-fuckin-gold and watching as a savage carved your beating heart from your chest.

Thanks to his leadership, his boys were good. Real good. So good, in fact, that he often thought of himself more as an exterminator than a soldier. But that was only because he had thoroughly educated his men in the order of things. No matter how trivial, opportunities to reinforce that order were never wasted. That was how he had become a god, and that was how he would stay one.

"If ya have any money left to pay her, Brown, ya can have her when I'm done." Lefty stared around the table. "Now, let's get this over with."

"Yer too eager, Cap'n," Brown said, eyebrows arched. "Makes a man wonder what's up yer sleeve."

"Brown, you know damn well what's up my sleeve, an' if ya say another word I'll gladly use it on ya." Lefty somehow squeezed the words through gritted teeth.

"He means his Derringer," Dingo noted.

Brown relented with a nod and sheepish grin. He took a bite from a hunk of crusty bread and chewed obnoxiously.

Dingo gestured to his chips already at the center of the table. Bull and Brown looked at each other, then shrugged, then pushed their smaller piles of chips forward.

When the cards were down, Lefty took the pot with four deuces. His men groaned and traced their undoing back to Uma's misleading comment which she construed as an honest mistake, two being such a low number and all. They never even thought to question how it was that Lefty came to possess all four twos in the first place. He scraped the winnings to his side of the table and tossed the remaining chunk of bread back to Stickman.

3

Magnus had emerged from the forest into a field of horseless wagons, and the remuda was nowhere to be found. It took him three days to reach Sagebrush Junction on foot. Standing in the dark outside the hairy wooden walls of the Withered Lizard Saloon, he heard men conversing, guffawing, and attempting to carry a tune. He could hear the tinny ringing of frayed piano wires and the doleful voice of a woman who sang much better than the whooperups. Despite the revelry, Magnus' mind dwelt on the pelts he desperately needed and the monsters that stood in his way.

The chilly breeze delivered a tangy whiff of vomit. *Lovely.* He glared through a valance of disheveled eyebrow at the saloon's inscrutable windows, their cloudy surface awash with the glow of burning lanterns. Dark forms swayed within. The people he would encounter inside made him nervous, but he had grown desperate. "A means to an end," he reminded himself. He brushed the dust from his suit, then sauntered up the steps and through the saloon doors.

Most of the patrons inside the Withered Lizard were uniformed soldiers, but he knew they would be. It's precisely why he had come. Yesterday afternoon he had happened by a traveling peddler on the east bank of the Croop Creek Bridge. The man was standing on the mucky shore, shirtless, the hem of his pants rolled above the knee, shaving his face. When he saw Magnus, he stopped and issued a well-rehearsed smile that seemed to engage every muscle in his face. *By George, it's the muse of comedy*, Magnus thought. The man toweled the white foam from his bulldog jaw and gestured to his cart in the shade of a cottonwood tree.

His smile faded as quickly as it had appeared when he learned that, no, Magnus was not interested in purchasing a polished tea kettle, or a new pair of boots, or a wide-brimmed sun hat perfect for long walks such as the one he was undertaking, or a gen-u-wine hardwood abacus, or an authentic Japanese Samurai sword, or even cartridges sure to put down anything that walked on four legs and squatted in the woods.

Unless Mister "High-Quality Holbrook" could tell him where to find soldiers, Magnus would kindly be on his way. Clearly disappointed but ever the salesman, Mister Holbrook told him that the Withered Lizard Saloon was the only place within a hundred miles he would find the men he sought—only he wouldn't call them soldiers anymore, not exactly—and that the ones he'd find there might just be the best he'd find in a radius ten times that.

Having finally arrived in the saloon, Magnus now laid eyes on the not-exactly soldiers. The remaining patrons were vagrants, whores, drunkards, and tired tradesmen, save one. A young Native man with a long face and gradual nose stood in the corner wearing a dog collar around his neck. His brown overalls and bare feet befitted a youth, but his bald head and boney frame aged him. He was perhaps seventeen, and…were his eyes *white*?

Ah, blind, which may have explained the collar around his neck.

Magnus drew a cleansing breath and inspected his suit. All the buttons were fastened. His pocket watch was not dangling around for all to see. His puff tie was properly…puffed. He looked up to find that everyone was staring. The room had fallen silent, even the piano.

Magnus cleared his throat. "Greetings! My name is Magnus Lief, and I am on a quest for pelts."

"Boys," said a soldier with captains' insignia, "pelt the man."

At once, glasses, bottles, boots, and even a ladies' undergarment took flight. He dodged all but two glasses, and by God's grace the undergarment fell short. He straightened himself and smoothed the wrinkles from his suit.

"Delightful," he said with a nervous chuckle. "I'm glad you're all so spirited. We're going to need that!"

"The hell you want, Moneybags?" asked a lieutenant.

"Men."

The room erupted with laughter, and Magnus felt heat rush into his cheeks.

"No," said Magnus. "No, no. Not like that. I need help acquiring my pelts."

"An' why would we do that?" asked a huge, bespectacled soldier whose rank was hidden beneath a harlot's lacy arms.

Magnus snorted. "Because you'll be handsomely rewarded."

The large, gibfaced soldier looked to the captain and meaning passed between them. The captain cocked an eyebrow, took his glass, and slugged what remained.

"I'm inclined to agree with Bull. I don't know ya, Mr. Lief, an' I don't like your look. Sounds like ya need trappers, anyway. Try the hotel two doors over."

Magnus drew back, contemplating the rejection. "Well …what of duty then?"

"What of it?" snarled a lieutenant, rising from his seat.

The captain tapped the table with his index finger. "Easy, Dingo," he said, and the lieutenant sank back onto his chair. "What Dingo means is that we ain't at your service, Mr. Lief. Ain't our duty to please you."

"Who delivers your orders then? I'll speak to him—"

"You're speakin to him now," the captain snapped.

"Surely you have superiors—"

"Surely I do not." The words punched forth, backed by a tempestuous glare.

Magnus withered, considering further discourse. He settled on a parting entreaty. "We have gotten off on the wrong foot. I meant no disrespect; I am desperate. The pelts I require are through a forest full of dangerous animals. Without the assistance of…capable men such as yourselves I will certainly perish—" the soldiers were unmoved "—my immense fortune dying with me. A terrible waste. I only ask for your consideration." He paused, satisfied by the subtle raising of brows at the mention of his fortune. He bowed. "Forgive my intrusion, gentlemen. Please resume your revelry."

The saloon was silent as he parted the swinging doors. His appeals to adventure, duty, and chivalry had failed. Ultimately, greed was their fuel oil. He had known it before entering the saloon, but he now had their full measure.

— ∴ —

In the ground floor bar of the Cielo Azul Inn, Magnus sat at a small round table opposite a gruff but amiable man named Otto Thibodeaux. A reek of cedar and polish and whiskey swirled in his nostrils. The grandfather clock in the lobby had read quarter past midnight when he arrived twenty minutes earlier, but despite the hour they weren't alone. Over Thibodeaux's shoulder and through open French doors, Magnus observed the inn's lanky proprietor hunched over the front desk. Other than to scribble in his ledger or claw at his mop of stringy white hair, the old man hadn't moved a muscle since assisting Magnus with the purchase of a flask of whiskey. His pencil swirled with grace, and since the man had yet to turn a single page, Magnus guessed he was drawing rather than tending the books. Innkeeper by day, artist by night, both lice infested.

The few lulls in Magnus' negotiations with the head of the trapping outfit were occupied by pencil murmurs and clock tocks. Thibodeaux was a sociable fellow, and when they weren't discussing terms he was gushing about his wife and daughters down on the Oklahoma homestead, the young kid in the outfit who reminded him of the son he still hoped to have, and the windpump he planned to build when he next returned home.

Thibodeaux smiled, a pleasant expression of upturned lips and all but two teeth, which was impressive for a man his age. After what Magnus had seen, any mouth with over ninety percent of the little cogs of digestion might as well be a full mouth. To what degree they had yellowed was a different question entirely.

The big man reached across the table and Magnus reciprocated, his hand disappearing into the scratchy womb of Thibodeaux's grip.

"This was fine timing, Mister Lief. We was just hittin a slump. Was thinkin 'bout headin north."

"It seems fortune has favored us both," Magnus said. "You're certain you and your men will be ready to depart by noon tomorrow? Time is of the essence."

"Swear it, sir, may God strike me dead."

Bang!

Thibodeaux jumped in his chair at the hateful noise from the lobby. Clutching his chest, he twisted away then back to Magnus. "That a damned gun?"

"I believe it was the front door slamming open." Magnus watched Thibodeaux's hand ease onto his revolver's grip. The trapper looked over his shoulder just as the captain strode in followed closely by his lieutenant who stopped to stand guard at the bar's French doors.

The captain stood off the trapper's shoulder and said, "Changed our minds. We wanna help with your pelts."

Magnus frowned. "Too late, I'm afraid. I've struck a deal with Mister Thibodeaux."

Measuring Thibodeaux with his eyes, the captain

scoffed. "That so? If what ya said about dangerous animals is true, ya need soldiers more than trappers. We're the best of both. While Tibby-doe here has been playin paddy-whack with beavers an' coons, me an' my men have been trappin the most dangerous beasts on earth."

"Indian women and children?" Thibodeaux smirked.

The captain's head spun toward the trapper.

Magnus interjected. "Mister Thibodeaux and I already shook on it." He pulled a coin from his pocket, tossed it to the captain. It caught the lanterns' glow flip after golden flip. "For your trouble."

The captain seized the coin and inspected it, eyes sparkling with avarice. "Shoulda led with this, Mister Lief." He looked up and stuck out his left hand. "Call me Lefty. Offer accepted."

"Deal's done," grunted Thibodeaux. "Go to hell!"

In a blur, the captain grabbed Thibodeaux by his wavy black hair, yanking his head back. Magnus' muscles seized. He sat frozen as a gun fired beneath the table, then another fired nearby. Glass shattered across the room. Magnus turned then looked back and Lefty was dragging a blade across Thibodeaux's throat.

Frozen, Magnus watched Thibodeaux flop in his chair momentarily before he finally stilled.

"That was unnecessary!" Magnus shouted over the ringing in his ears.

"You made it necessary," came Lefty's muffled reply. The captain wiped the blade on Thibodeaux's shoulder, then gestured to the door. "After you, Mister Lief."

Magnus rose, the tinnitus subsiding. It was replaced by

clomping footfalls, slamming doors, and a crying baby. Lefty glared at Magnus, then grabbed him by the puff tie and slung him toward the open French doors where the lieutenant stood guard.

"Get the men," Lefty shouted.

Magnus blinked, and Dingo was already outside.

At the doorway to the lobby Magnus was yanked back by his collar. Lefty stepped ahead and posted up, drawing his sword and raising it overhead. Footsteps thumped down the stairs. Adrenaline spiraled through Magnus and some basic instinct made him shrink back.

A gun slunk around the door frame in the grip of a hairy arm. Lefty wrapped the arm against his side, twisted, and ran his sword through the man's chest. As the man fell, Lefty drew his revolver and leaned through the door, aiming upstairs.

"Now's a good time to move, Mister Lief."

Magnus faltered.

"Get outside, dammit!"

Magnus scurried past the captain and through the lobby realizing when he saw the innkeeper slumped over the front desk that the second shot he heard had been Dingo's. A shotgun had replaced the pencil in the old man's hand, but the ledger remained open beside him. On the top page was a drawing that Magnus recognized as the inn's facade. Gunshots exploded from behind. He snatched the ledger, slipped it into his vest, broke into a panicked sprint, and burst forth into the night chased by the screams of wounded men.

Leaping from the porch, Magnus traversed the deeply

rutted mud toward a disheveled formation of drunken mercenaries. Under the new deal, he supposed those were his soldiers. He reached the men and spun to find Lefty only a few steps behind, marching swiftly toward his company. He passed Magnus then stopped to address Dingo and a jittery young corporal.

"Dingo, take a dozen men 'round back. We're gonna smoke—"

A gunshot rang out from the hotel and the young corporal's breathing hitched. Confusion washed over him. His eyes bugged, and he sank down, clawing at a swelling dark spot on his chest. Magnus crouched and spun around to spy a silhouette in a second story window. A thunderous cacophony of gunfire commenced, and Magnus covered his ears but did not look away. The window disintegrated into sparkling sand. The walls became a cloud of mulch. The air whipped into a froth of gun smoke, dust, and blood.

Lefty whistled, raised his hand, and the gunfire ceased. "Smokey, Gimp." Two soldiers stepped forward. "Burn it."

The dense words rapped against Magnus' ears.

As Smokey trotted and Gimp…gimped toward the hotel's entrance, Lefty muttered something to Dingo who then led his dozen around back. Smokey and Gimp reached the front porch and took the lanterns from their hooks.

"Shoot anyone that tries to escape," Lefty yelled to the remaining soldiers.

Then, he whistled.

The men threw the lanterns against the door and their flames devoured it. Smokey jumped back, cursing, and Gimp staggered away swatting his smoldering pants.

Tongues of warm air licked Magnus' face. "There's no need for this, Captain. The job is yours!"

Lefty turned slowly, his hard jade eyes cut low beneath his brow. "Ain't about the job. This here's a lesson, and they ain't learned it yet."

"You're not teaching anyone anything, you're just *killing*," Magnus said. "And I'm quite sure the families inside don't deserve that!"

Lefty nodded toward his soldiers. "Lesson's for them. Let the trappers live, and they'll round up a posse an' track us to the end of the earth. Blood for blood. That's how it works 'round here. Ain't no room for half measures in this life. It's have or have not, take or get took, kill or be killed. Witnesses will send ya to the gallows; your own mercy ties the noose."

The flames engulfed the center of the hotel, consuming the wooden shingles up to the ridge. At the near end, a window shattered, and a man climbed out onto the first-floor eave. He reached back and a woman extended a bundle of blankets out the window. A tiny arm dangled from its folds. The man took the bundle and the woman climbed out, nearly losing her balance. A little girl in a nightgown followed. She was crying and clutching a stuffed rabbit in the crook of her arm.

Magnus turned and addressed Lefty's men. "What if that was your family?"

The young gangly soldier who had sat at Lefty's card

game spat at Magnus' feet and said, "What if you's a fuckin' extra-tera-sterile?"

Magnus cringed at the man's rotting teeth. "What did you say?"

Lefty grabbed Magnus by the throat, fingers digging in. "Extra-terrestrial. It's Brown's new word. He's sayin' *what if* and *what ain't* don't matter, only what *is*. We're alive an' free, and that's how we'll stay. We'll kill the whole god-damn town if we have to. And if you attempt to influence my men again I'll string you up by your pebbles."

Lefty pushed Magnus down and whistled, and his men took aim. Magnus looked away and plugged his ears as they unleashed hell. His gaze fell on the young Native man in the dog collar. His white eyes conveyed the inferno's deadly light, and golden rills glistened down his cheeks.

Breaks in the gunfire brought screaming and moaning, and laughter from the men. More gunfire thundered behind the inn, and more screams, and more laughter. As the body count climbed, Magnus grew certain that High-Quality Holbrook had been right. These were the perfect men for the job.

4

Lefty's rogue company didn't produce any new corpses in the two days following the massacre, which was nice. They had reached the terrible forest's edge in the twilight of a pink and purple sunset that flared from some hopeful place beyond the looming mountain with its jagged conifer hem.

Against Magnus' advice, they made camp on the prairie only a stone's throw from those conspiring trees. Magnus sat at one of two fires as tall as a man. They raged so hotly it was a wonder the whole field hadn't suffered the same fate as Bull's eyebrows when the wood first ignited. Soldiers sat on rocks or stumps or matted grass, some already dozing on their bed rolls. Large, murky forms lumbered at the brink of the flickering light. It was the hobbled horses and Magnus knew it, but each shifting shadow still raised his hackles.

Magnus sipped tea from his tin mug and searched the depths between trunks for glowing eyes until his own began to ache. He blinked, rubbed the burning, itching orbs, and surveyed the soldiers, lingering again on Brown's awful teeth. "Is that why they call you Brown?"

"Because of his teeth?" Lefty asked.

The men laughed.

"That ain't it," Brown started. "So, I's scalpin this Injin, sawin hard, an' he's squirmin. With all his fussin I almost took my damn thumb off, so I stab em with my knife an' finish the scalpin, but by then I's thirsty as a humpless camel an' I see this jug in the corner of the hut that looks for drinkin. Sure as shootin it got somethin wet inside that smells like whiskey. I love whiskey, so I drink the whole damn thing. Ain't even a half hour before it hits me—"

Magnus cringed. "It wasn't whiskey?"

Brown shook his head and blew snot from his left nostril. "Milk from the devil's teat, far as I know. I spent the ride back paintin a white horse brown."

The men laughed as Bull added, "The only thing trottin faster than the horse was Brown's backdoor!" With this, the soldiers doubled over, slapped knees, stomped the ground. A look around the campfire confirmed that several had laughed themselves breathless.

Magnus grimaced and, eager to move on, turned to the chuckling lieutenant. "Why are you Dingo?"

Dingo removed his hat and ran his finger along a lumpy pale fissure in his black hair. "Had lice when I was ten. Mama coated my head with bacon grease thinkin it would kill the critters an' I got attacked by a pack of mangy dogs on the way to school. Damn near scalped me. Got rid of the lice though."

"Really, the bacon grease worked?" Magnus asked.

"No. Doc Nelson shaved me bald to sew my head." Dingo simpered.

"A tried and true solution, to be sure, but you didn't really answer my question."

Bull said, "A feller from Australia rode with us a while back. He heard that story and called him Dingo. It stuck."

Magnus nodded slowly at the bespectacled man. "It's obvious why you're Bull. All you're missing are the horns."

Bull held his fists to the sides of his head with pinkies raised. He bellowed like a beast, and everyone laughed.

A flash of movement came from Brown as the soldier shouted, "Here, Stickman, eat this."

Something stirred in the grass behind Magnus. He turned and saw the blind young man sitting against a wagon wheel with his legs drawn up.

"Brown, that better not be a rabbit turd," the captain warned from the other side of the fire.

"Ain't no turd, Cap'n, it's a *flower*." The final word came out with mock delicacy.

Magnus watched Stickman feel the ground in search of what had struck his leg. He found the flower and picked it up, holding it at eye level and stroking the petals before popping it into his mouth. Magnus turned to the men and asked, "Why do you call him Stickman?"

Lefty sighed and pointed with his knife. "Found him in a pueblo in Oklahoma tappin everything with a stick. Got the harness now so he don't need the stick, but he'll always be the stick man."

"Stickman," Magnus repeated vacantly. He looked through the flames at Lefty who returned to cleaning his nails with a knife. "You're left-handed."

"That so?" Lefty asked, green eyes focused on his nails.

It grew quiet and Magnus watched him before asking, "Why bother?"

"What, cleanin' my nails? Only thing that separates us from the animals. We eat anything an' everything. We kill anything an' everything. We fuck anything an' everything. Clean nails is all that's left."

Magnus contemplated. "You wear clothes."

"Not always. B'sides, what are feathers an' fur if not the clothes of the animal kingdom?"

Magnus snorted. "You have a dangerous way of making sense out of nonsense."

Lefty's thin lips curled, and a snaggletooth poked out. He sipped his drink and said, "You got a nose for nonsense, do ya?"

"I have been known to sniff it out."

"I got somethin ya can sniff," Brown quipped. The men chuckled.

Lefty ignored them. "Doubtful. You don't even recognize the nonsense starin' ya in the face."

"And that would be?"

"This place. When you wanted soldiers for trappin, I knew ya were comin here. You don't think we've heard the stories 'bout this mountain, these woods?" Lefty waved an arm toward the tree line. "I'm guessin you heard 'em too, only you were fool enough to believe there's monsters out there."

Magnus surveyed the sneering skeptics. Heads nodded. "Well, if it's all the same to you, I'd still feel better under your protection. I'm happy to pay."

Lefty snickered. "Oh, we're *gonna* take your money to fend off the squirrels, Mr. Lief. We knew it'd be an easy payoff. It's why we took the job."

"Mmhmm, easy," Magnus agreed to himself.

Bull adjusted his glasses and leaned forward, elbows on knees. "The part I can't figure out is what kinda pelts are worth paying fifty men to protect you from furry forest animals."

Magnus drew a deep breath and held it, measuring the pressure in his chest. "Have you heard of the tedekar?"

Lefty released a pained groaned.

"Everybody's heard of a tedekar," said Dingo. "They ain't real."

"Oh, I can assure you they're real," Magnus said. "They're the most beautiful creatures you'll ever see. In the sunlight, their golden fur sparkles so brightly it's nearly blinding. To run your fingers through it is to feel something so fine and soft that everything else is straw by comparison. It's worth a fortune, and that's just the pelt. Their oil is a sweet, musky perfume, a single spritz known to last a week without fading. Boiling their bones produces a medicinal broth potent enough to cure cholera, scarlet fever, and diphtheria. When powdered and mixed with water, their claws produce an adhesive that prevents infection—ideal for treating battlefield wounds. They're the most valuable creatures on the planet and—" he paused dramatically "—I've found a whole herd."

They hung on Magnus' words, eyes sparkling with greed. All except Lefty whose skeptical gaze bored into Magnus. After a beat, he huffed and refocused on his nails.

Brown asked, "If you knows where they is, how come you ain't killed one for proof?"

"How come, indeed." Magnus sighed. "Tedekar are

elusive, far too quick for an old man to hunt alone. Even if I could catch one, they're ill-tempered things—"

"I ain't never seen one at the market," Dingo blurted.

Magnus chuckled. "Do you shop alongside presidents and kings?"

Dingo snorted. "No."

"That's why you've never seen one," Magnus said matter-of-factly. "But that'll change once we've succeeded."

A clap came, then another. Lefty applauded Magnus with zero enthusiasm. "Mr. Lief, if these pelts don't work out you got a future in sales, I'll give ya that. O'course, if we don't come out of this with the fortune you're promisin, you won't have a future at all." He spat and lifted his tin mug in a menacing toast.

Magnus swallowed hard. Whatever meaning the captain intended, he was correct. If Magnus failed to secure his pelts, the future was bleak indeed.

— ∴ —

Lefty undid his fly and extracted his member through the fabric folds. "Dingo, get over here," he called in a stifled yell.

He faced a tree trunk just barely within the fires' diminished light. It had been hours since they made camp, and the men were now asleep except for Brown—he was on first watch with Lefty, and Dingo—who had been cleaning his side arm. Lief was also still awake, but he hardly counted as a man. He had been sitting by the fire, flipping the pages of a picture book when Lefty arose. Any simpleton who believed in tedekar *would* enjoy a good children's book.

Warm currents massaged his neck, releasing his bladder's chokehold. Pain sliced its way down his urethra until it broke free in a mustard-colored stream. Odd that it was actually urine; he half expected sandburs. *Damn you, Uma.*

The field behind him swished with prudent strides that Lefty recognized as Dingo's even before he arrived at his left flank. But there came another set of walking sounds, ungainly and aloof. Brown.

The young corporal sidled up on Lefty's right until their shoulders were touching. "I knows ya wasn't makin water without me." He proceeded to unclip his suspenders and drop his pants all the way to his ankles. "Hmm, you feel that? The fire's smoochin my ass cheeks. Pecker's cold as a walrus tusk though, an' my hands ain't helpin that none."

Dingo leaned into Lefty's peripheral vision. "Brown, shut yer trap."

Brown's jaw snapped shut and his eyes flicked between Dingo and Lefty.

Lefty glowered back. "Splash me an' I'll bleed ya out."

Brown's Adam's apple bobbed.

"Orders, sir?" Dingo prodded.

Lefty met the conspiratorial gaze of a man who knew why he was summoned.

If anyone in the company was a younger version of himself it was Dingo. He'd be lying if he said he felt no fondness for the boy. It'd be a real shame if he ever had to kill his trusty lieutenant. Dingo was shrewd, but he wasn't particularly intelligent, which benefited him. If he had been both shrewd and intelligent, Lefty would have killed him already.

But this wasn't about Dingo.

In a grave whisper, Lefty said, "In case ya haven't figured it out, we're gonna have to kill Mister Lief b'fore this is over."

Dingo pursed his lips and nodded. "I figured."

"I didn't," Brown admitted. "We ain't gonna do it til after we gets the tedekar, right?"

"Tedekar ain't real, dimwit," Dingo snapped.

Lefty shook and stuffed himself back into his pants. Buttoning up, he said, "I'm glad to hear ya say that, Dingo. I thought you were buying that horse shit."

"I was only smilin in the end b'cause he made it all sound so fantastical, but I didn't b'lieve it. He's a slippery son of a bitch."

"So when we doin it?" Brown asked, crouching to retrieve his pants.

"We'll give him a day. I'll admit I'm curious to see what he's draggin us all out here for." Dingo and Brown nodded. "Don't neither of ya say nothin to anyone."

Brown twisted over his shoulder, turned back. "What about Bull?"

"Bull's book smart, but he ain't got no common sense. I'd wager he an' several others b'lieve Mister Lief, an' the promise of fortune always wins converts. Just keep it quiet til I give the order. When I do, make it quick—no warning, just a bullet to the back of the head."

Brown smiled, raised his hand in the shape of a gun, pointed it at Dingo's head, and fired. "Bang."

5

Magnus flipped another page in the innkeeper's ledger to a depiction of a cardinal perched atop a wooden post. The detail was remarkable. He could see the cornified folds of its legs, the feathers' overlapping barbules, and even the subtle striations on its beak. Every page had contained a drawing so lifelike that it filled Magnus with wonder, and the deeper he penetrated the book, the greater their fidelity became. It would be reasonable to assume that the innkeeper's ability had been improving with practice, but Magnus could see the same adept pencil strokes in all the images. The differentiating factor, he surmised, had been time, and the drawing that exhibited the most patience and care was yet unfinished. It was a portrait of a woman that grew more unrefined the farther right he looked. Magnus' heart sank as he examined it and thought of Ingrid. The woman wasn't her, but they shared some ineffable quality that connected them.

Someone called for Dingo. Magnus watched the lieutenant pop up and walk toward the forest. A second later Brown followed. He considered eavesdropping on them when something stirred in the grass behind him—Stickman, surely. He glanced over his shoulder and Stickman scrambled back, raising his dirty palms as a shield. Magnus raised his own in a gesture of peace. "I apologize, friend. I didn't mean to spook you."

Stickman shrugged and lowered his arms propping them on his knees.

"That's right. You don't speak English." Magnus snorted at himself.

"A little," Stickman rasped.

Multiple realizations dawned on Magnus at once. Not only could Stickman speak English, he understood it quite well. More astonishing was the revelation that those cloudy eyes were not entirely unseeing. Had he not intentionally approached Magnus then fallen back when he saw Magnus turn?

Magnus looked around. Satisfied no one was watching, he motioned Stickman closer. "You can see," he whispered, pointing to his eyes.

"A little."

Hopefully he knows more English than that, Magnus thought. His extensive travels had supplied him with a rudimentary vocabulary in a dozen languages, but he was far from fluent in any of them and had found that speaking only some of a language could be worse than speaking none at all.

"They think you're blind," Magnus said, covering his eyes with his hand.

Stickman responded in a blend of English and his native tongue, and Magnus recognized enough of the language that he was able to understand the young man's meaning: "Do not tell. They will kill me."

"I won't." Magnus' heart faltered at the danger Stickman had endured. Against all prudence, a rogue notion found utterance. "Shall I free you?"

Stickman shook his head.

"No?" The incredulous response came out louder than intended. He surveyed the sleeping men who seemed not to notice, hushing his voice anew. "Why on Earth not?"

Stickman lowered his gaze, searched the ground, and found a word. "Sister." He went on to explain through gesticulation and linguistic intersection that Lefty had sold his little sister, Itamah, into slavery and was the only one who might know her whereabouts. Stickman had suffered months in Lefty's captivity with the hope of someday finding her.

Magnus placed a hand on Stickman's shoulder and his eyes gleamed, but his gaze was focused on Magnus' lap. Stickman had spied the innkeeper's ledger. He extended an open hand and said, "Please." Despite being nearly blind, even he could appreciate the artistry. He handed the book to the doomed young man and turned back to the fire.

"Bang!" someone shouted near the woods, and snide laughter followed.

Magnus looked for the source of the sound and soon witnessed three men birthed from the shadows into the wavering orange glow. Dingo. Lefty. Brown. Never had he seen a more untrustworthy trio. Their mischievous grins filled him with foreboding. He snatched the ledger from Stickman, who scrambled away, then turned to scrutinize their perverted glee. A dreadful picture began to form.

Before Magnus could arrive at any actionable conclusions, his eyes were drawn upward to the forest's saw-toothed silhouette. Several trees stood taller than the rest and swayed strangely—inverted pendulums wiping away the stars. There was no wind, yet they pitched side to side as if riding a gale.

Silence.

Magnus' skin prickled at the realization that the evening's chorus of chirping crickets had ceased. Lefty, Dingo, and Brown's rustling steps were the only sounds on the entire earth. Then one of the treetops did something he had never seen before. It unfurled itself, stretching its branches as if to take flight. Impossibly, it did just that. The treetop leapt upward, the wings drove down, and it took to the air as a black and frightful specter.

"Captain," Magnus called. He lost track of the silhouette against the night sky, and as he scanned, he noticed more treetops spreading their wings. Fear exploded through his body, a shockwave rippling from cell to cell. "Lefty! Something's coming!"

A shape swooped low over the fire shrieking like some prehistoric beast, and the flames whipped in its wake. Beyond the light's reach, a horse screamed. The remuda shuffled and grunted, and a second scream came. The soldiers scrambled for their guns and formed a perimeter, muzzles trained outward in all directions.

"What's happening?" someone yelled.

More primal shrieks came from the sky. Shadows darted overhead.

Nearby, Brown yelled, "It's too dark! Cain't see a fuckin thing!"

The ground trembled with two immense thuds, sparks and smoke swirled through the camp, and darkness closed in. Magnus spun. The campfires were smothered beneath horse carcasses.

"Better, Brown?" someone quipped.

Turning back toward the encroaching abyss, Magnus fought panic to blink long and hard, erasing the embers' afterimage.

"Get them lanterns lit!" barked Lefty.

Amid the scurrying and metallic clinking Magnus felt the air stir around his face—a sudden puff, then stillness. Footsteps approached from straight ahead. He squinted, strained, bid his eyes to see. The mountain brome rustled, and as the sound drew closer, there was a series of staccato pips and squeaks. Gooseflesh rippled over his every inch. His arm hair stood stiff. Whatever was coming was nearly upon him. Was that breath against his cheek? He saw nothing through the night's impenetrable veil.

Finally, the lanterns came to life and their soft yellow light fell upon a bizarre waddling creature. The bald and wrinkled vampire bat stood at least four feet tall, its wingspan double that. A pair of goat horns crowned its head, and above its rather small mouth with a hundred needle-like teeth was a pointy, upturned nose. It toddled toward Magnus, clicking and squeaking, ogling him with dimpled black eyes.

With a hiss it halted and began to wiggle on the spot. Two more creatures materialized out of the darkness behind the first. They waddled forward, clicking and squeaking like demented children.

"Should we shoot?" The soldier's voice quivered.

Magnus' face wrenched. "*Now* you hesitate?"

forward, glancing toward the roiling sky that seemed oblivious to his presence…until his next movement struck something metal. The resulting clatter might as well have been a dinner bell. A dimly lit face eventually emerged beneath the wagon. It had a small, square chin, a long nose, sharp cheeks, and a pair of dull white eyes. Stickman.

Magnus glanced skyward then scrambled toward the wagon. He reached the undercarriage and placed a hand on Stickman's shoulder. "It's me, Stickman. I'm here."

Stickman said, "We go."

"No. Bad idea. This is the safest place." Magnus tuned his ears to the forest, listening for screams or gunfire, hearing none. Perhaps he should have followed the soldiers. Perhaps they still could.

"What is happening?" Stickman asked.

"There's a cloud of bats above us, human height, with horns, mouthfuls of fangs, swordlike talons, and huge fleshy wings. They've killed a half dozen men already."

"They kill Lefty's men?"

"Yes."

"Good bats."

"But you need them to find your sister," Magnus noted.

Stickman's eyes rounded into cue balls. He hadn't considered this.

Magnus sighed. "And I still need my pelts. We need them alive, which is ironic; I believe they plan to kill me."

Stickman hung his head. After a moment, he craned his neck and set his gaze up beyond the wagon's edge.

Magnus looked out toward the meadow where the campfires' scattered embers still flickered. It was as if small holes had been punched in the earth's shell allowing the orange light of its great firebox to peek through. Such a morbid machine, the earth, determined to run on blood when wine would do just fine. Magnus longed for the day he would move on from this brutal rock, if only to float in the infinite darkness of the universe.

The wagon lurched as if burdened by a runaway boulder. Its springs issued an awful shriek. Stickman shrunk back as Magnus crept forth, turning his gaze upward. Talons pierced the sideboards and beyond them peered down a bat's gore encrusted head. It ogled him with large, curious eyes. The wagon lurched again, and then two more times in quick succession. Magnus' pulse faltered with each impact.

From somewhere in the woods men screamed and volleys of gunfire erupted. They were saved! Lefty and his men had seen the bats on the wagon and were coming to the rescue! But the gunfire sounded different. It was softer, and there was no zipping or snapping as he had heard when the settlers shot past him. Lefty's men were shooting the other way, *into* the woods.

The bats spread their wings. Membranes of flesh rustled like canvas in the wind. They drove downward, and with each powerful flap a cyclone of dust abraded Magnus' face. He closed his eyes. When he opened them again, the wagon was overhead and still climbing. From a spoke trailed a leather strap, and at the end of that strap stood his young friend, Stickman. He was on his toes, tugging at the rapidly tightening leash.

Magnus' thoughts tumbled and leapt side to side, under

and over. There were dogs that did such maneuvers. He had seen it at the circus in St. Louis. What a strange lot. One man had even stepped into a ring with a lion! Stickman needed such a man now, one undeterred by heinous beasts.

Magnus felt his courage multiply, his muscles invigorate.

He pushed up and scrambled to Stickman, going straight for the neck and feeling the collar for a buckle. His fingers dragged over a row of rivets, then a metal band. The collar was a permanent fixture. Magnus scoured the ground for a knife, a pot, a rock, anything he could weaponize. His efforts returned wads of grass and a blanket. Hadn't Bull fallen somewhere to his left? He would have weapons. Magnus turned and crawled, sweeping his hands along the ground.

He kept an eye on Stickman as he probed forward. The leash was nearly taut, the wagon still ascending. Just then Magnus felt Bull's shoulder. He patted down to the man's waist, found his knife's handle, and withdrew it from its sheath. Its grip was a club, its heft surprising. He spun to find the wagon almost ten feet off the ground. Below, Stickman hung by his neck. He wriggled like a fish on a line, clawing at the collar, trying to pull himself up on the leather strap that was tighter than a fiddle string.

Something unfamiliar activated within Magnus: compassion. He had seen men hanged in Philadelphia. He had seen crippled children begging in Chicago. He had seen families sleeping in the alleyways of New Orleans. But none of that touched him this way. For years Stickman had suffered the cruelty of a dim world, for months he had endured the brutality of his captors, and he was still the most decent of them all. Stickman's story couldn't end this way.

Magnus broke into a full sprint. Leaping as he reached the cart, his fingers wrapped around the felloe of the nearest wheel. He hung there beside Stickman and flailed at the leather strap with Bull's knife. The blade slapped crookedly several times before its edge finally bit, and after a few seconds of frantic sawing what was left of the leash stretched and snapped.

Stickman hit the ground and Magnus dropped beside him.

"Come, Stickman," said Magnus as he grabbed him under the arm.

They ran for the trees, stumbling through the brush. But they only made it part way before someone's shout cut through the gunfire. "Get down!"

The ferocity in the voice quashed all hesitation, and Magnus fell forward into the dirt pulling Stickman down with him. Gunfire banged away at the tree line. Rounds buzzed low over Magnus' head. From above there was a meaty *thump* and pained squawk. A bat crashed to the earth at his left, and there came more screeching and the snapping of bones.

"Come, Lief! Stay low," Lefty ordered.

Magnus stood and pulled Stickman up. They ran ahead, ducking when something large cut through the sky and crashed against the trees—the wagon. Soldiers grunted and fell back as a flapping ceiling of flesh, talons, and teeth descended on the meadow. The relative safety of the trees stood only yards away. They could make it. They *had* to make it. Magnus sprinted onward and Stickman stumbled in tow, hand firmly in Magnus' grasp. Behind, the clamor grew as the bats closed posthaste.

He urged Stickman on. He would not fail him.

The wretch was one of the only people with whom Magnus had interacted for any length of time without feeling revulsion. He might even admire the young man. He would do everything he could to protect him, the least of which was to keep running, but Stickman wasn't making it easy. Magnus glanced back just as a diving wraith took shape to the rear.

A gun discharged beside Magnus' head. In an instant the bat's face imploded, and it fell from the sky.

Ringing was all Magnus heard for the eternity that followed. That was it, he was deaf, his good deed properly punished. What a sad pair he and Stickman would make. He spun into Lefty's glare who nodded toward the forest. They ran to the trees and traversed the wagon's wreckage, Lefty covering them, until they stood among the haggard soldiers.

Magnus didn't need ears to sense the curses being hurled his way.

Braced against a tree, he shook his head, worked his jaw, and tugged at his ears, and the *screeee* finally subsided. Voices seeped through, and words took shape.

"The hell is this place, tricky ol' imp?" Dingo barked.

"Brought us here to die!" yelled another.

There were other murmurings among the shouts, men

saying things like, "Spider's fangs was bigger than my pecker," to which another replied, "That ain't sayin much."

Ignoring them, Magnus turned his attention to Stickman. "Are you okay?"

"I am not hurt," Stickman answered, but Magnus checked the young man over anyway.

"Get another strap for Stickman," Lefty ordered no one in particular.

Then he twisted and sent his left fist hurtling into Magnus' right cheek. Pain boomed through Magnus' skull as his head snapped back. He staggered a step or two.

"You fuckin knew the stories was true! *That's* why ya asked soldiers b'fore trappers. Must've come here already."

Magnus said nothing as he regained his balance. He pressed a hand to his cheek and looked past Lefty to where a moose, *the* moose, lay slain. Soldiers' body parts adorned its rack.

Lefty leaned closer. "Every man dies out here is your doin, an' don't forget, it's blood for blood. I will collect your debt."

He spat and walked away barking orders at his soldiers. There were supplies in that field they couldn't leave behind even if their retrieval risked more lives. Magnus knew with dreadful certainty that more *would* die before the sun rose, and that even if they didn't, Lefty would eventually kill him anyway.

6

After a casualty-free operation recovering much of their ammo, a day's worth of rations and water, and a leather satchel about which Lefty was particularly adamant, Magnus led the company deeper into the forest. They skirted the spider holes—many were dead, having been killed during the soldiers' initial retreat into the trees—and they passed where Magnus first saw the moose. This was the farthest he had penetrated the woods, and the closest he had come to the crater. His heart lifted with the thought but sank with the remembrance of their dwindling numbers. What had started as almost fifty was now thirty-eight, and there was still much ground to cover.

At least their passage had grown easier. They had scarcely slowed since traversing a stretch of chest-high tree roots. There were fewer trees the farther they went, and only sparse vegetation grew between the enormous trunks and laden boughs. The hills were far from barren, but the aspens, cottonwoods, and poplars had quit the higher elevations, and the remaining conifers seemed pleased with the elbow room. Even their footing had improved on account of the shallower plant litter.

Though Magnus helmed the lanceolate formation, it was no position of honor, and it wasn't just the likelihood of being the first one eaten that spoiled the distinction. Reports of shifting shadows from the men were his only distraction from the niggling notion that there was a revolver aimed at the back of his head. Each time they grew too quiet, Magnus glanced back expecting just enough time to register the shape of that black bore before it spit flames through his face.

"Movement, three o'clock," called a voice from the rear of the company.

Magnus glanced that way to discover a bulky, towering shadow. A bear? His heart lurched and his muscles drew taut with potential. It was nearly ten seconds before he recognized it as a mountain hemlock of mere natural size. Amongst the giants there had stood such trees, especially as the elevation increased, but Magnus feared that would not be true of the wildlife.

He settled himself, but as he turned forward something glimmered near the base of that tree. Eyes. They winked out, and in their absence the hint of a form became visible. Its silhouette stood a half shade deeper than the surrounding murk, but Magnus could clearly make out the skitter of four legs until it moved behind the next tree.

Magnus raised his arm to point, but Lefty stepped up and blocked it down.

"Yeah, we're bein followed," Lefty said, his voice hushed. "Brandy already pointed that out."

"Shouldn't we do something?"

"Shoont we do sumtin?" Brown mocked from two strides back.

"*We?*" Lefty huffed. "That's rich. Do ya even know

- 46 -

what it is or how many there are or if it's even a threat? We cain't afford to waste ammo or pick a fight with a superior force when we ain't got the terrain in our favor. You ain't got sense enough to last ya through the night. Like grabbin that knife instead of a gun." Lefty was nearly shouting now, his passion revealing the thought he had invested in the matter. "Why not use Bull's gun? Coulda killed the bats liftin the wagon an' still had rounds to defend yourself across the meadow."

"I…" Magnus started but trailed off. He thought for a moment, then steeled himself for the ridicule that would follow. "I've never fired a gun."

Nearly every man stopped and stared in disbelief. A few aloof men bumped into the backs of those who stared. Laughter sprung up like bubbles from a tar pit, and within seconds everyone was overtaken by gleeful spasms at Magnus' expense. Everyone except Lefty, whose face was pinched with more lines than a Celtic knot. Magnus had never seen a more contemptuous look.

"Shut yer yaps!" Lefty spat over his shoulder and turned back to Magnus. "Why haven't ya fired a gun?"

"As I'm sure you've noticed," Magnus started with a humorless chuckle, "my appetite for violence is rather anorectic. I'd have no taste for it at all if not for matters of survival. Allowing that, I still see no sport in using a machine to kill with your little finger." Magnus raised his hand to eye level and worked his index finger in and out. "It's simply not fair."

"Out here it ain't sport, it *is* survival, and there ain't no such thing as a fair fight when your life's on the line. Ya think those beasts care about what's fair?"

"I don't suppose they've ever thought about it, but all they have at their disposal is what nature has given."

"Nature!" Lefty snapped. "Look around! Nothin 'bout these woods is natural. B'sides, it's in *our* nature to invent shit like guns."

Brown drew his revolver and gave it a twirl. "You's in the wrong place to not like guns." He snickered and kissed the barrel.

"I am well aware. If it were up to me I'd be far, far away from here, and while we're on the subject, we need to keep moving." Magnus walked away, leaving the conversation behind. After a few steps, the men followed. "I have a question for you, Captain. I've been trying to think of a good way to ask it, but there isn't one." Magnus paused, prepared himself. "You've presented your arguments, weak though they were, for why all your killing is necessary. If you truly believe what you say, why spare anyone?"

"You ain't askin 'bout just anyone. You mean the blind Indian."

"Yes, I mean Stickman." Magnus glanced back to where a soldier named Coal was leading Stickman by the leash. "His scalp would've claimed a bounty like all the others."

"You wouldn't understand, Lief, but Stickman is special to me." Lefty smirked. "I have big plans for the boy."

Magnus stepped over a fallen branch. "Ominous..."

"Ain't like that." Lefty snorted. "I reckon he's the one person who cain't never turn on me."

"Because he's blind?"

"That's right." Lefty said. "Ain't *him* who should be

worried." The implication was clear.

Magnus exhaled and rubbed the back of his neck. "No, I suppose that would be me."

"Right again."

"You should know that if you don't protect me, you won't get paid and your men will have died for no gain."

"Oh, we'll find a way to get paid."

"That wasn't my point, Captain."

"That's always the point, Lief."

They negotiated a steep slope into a deep gully.

Brown giggled behind them. "Ya scared, Lief?"

"Should be," Dingo added. "Between us and the monsters you ain't got a friend in the whole damn world."

"Most certainly true," Magnus conceded, looking over his shoulder, "but we don't have to be friends to remain civil, do we? Like it or not, we're allies until we emerge from these woods alive and loaded down with tedekar pelts."

Lefty stopped in the shallow runoff, an inch of burbling water diverting around his boots. The formation halted with him. "Allies, hmm?" His chin slid forward, head bobbing, and his brow creased pensively. "That's how ya see this?"

Magnus felt his face stiffen, unsure how to interpret Lefty's manner.

"Hey, Brown," Lefty called, "got a new word for ya."

"Not sure I's ready for another, Cap'n. Still havin fun with ex-trees-torrential."

"Extra-terrenstral," Dingo corrected.

A smile twiddled the corners of Magnus' mouth. "The

word is extra-terrestrial. As future tedekar tycoons, you would be well-served in mastering such vernacular if you're going to assimilate with your illustrious peers."

There was silence as the men exchanged quizzical glances.

"Shit, we gotta talk like that?" Dingo asked.

"I cain't learn French," Brown said.

Magnus' jaw slackened and he found himself glaring through his brow. "Brown...that was English."

"Bullshit. I knows French when I hears it."

"Brown, you're a fuckin moron, but you're right about bullshit. Lief's a flannel-mouthed leech, which leads me to your new word: parasitical. It describes somethin that survives by feedin off ya without makin a contribution of its own, just like Lief."

"Paratestical," Brown attempted.

Laughter roared through the ranks. Lefty hushed them, and they marched on.

As they splashed through the gully where the mountain rains and melting snow drained into the valley, something howled nearby. It was the baleful baying of a wolf, but the sound was dissonant with bitter harmonies. The men froze, heads swiveling for the sound's source. Shapes shifted in the darkness, darting between the trees along the gully's ridge. Their gentle padding would have been inaudible if not for the bed of tree litter that crunched with each nimble step.

"Out of this gully, men!" Lefty ordered. "Dingo, your squad is rearguard!"

Coal tossed Stickman's leash to another soldier and

joined Dingo, raising their weapons rearward. Magnus turned and charged with everyone else up the gully's far slope. When he crested the top, he nearly stuffed his face into a set of snapping jaws. Magnus yanked back, his weight pitching over center. He flailed, trying to regain his balance, and got a good look at the creature. It was a three-headed wolf. Its primary head was ordinary enough, but on either side was a malformed imitation lacking fur or ears. The shriveled pink heads with mouths of crooked teeth were held by long worm-like necks.

His flailing stopped. Butterflies danced in his stomach as he entered freefall. A hand latched onto his forearm. It yanked him up and around, spinning him away from the beast and onto flat ground. The face that greeted him was Lefty's. Magnus thought to thank him, but he was already pivoting to aim a revolver at the snarling beast.

The jaws of its right head snapped shut over Lefty's forearm before he could align his shot. Still he fired twice, bullets that were destined for some distant tree trunk. The gun fell from his grasp, as the foul creature's center head lunged forth with snapping jaws and flying spittle.

Yes, rip his arm off! Eat him alive! Magnus thought before chiding himself. The pelts. He still needed these men, and they weren't worth a damn without Lefty. Magnus dove for the gun and rolled under the wolf. Pressing the muzzle beneath its center head, he pulled the trigger.

The revolver bucked violently, and the wolf collapsed on top of him, its weight forcing the air from his lungs. Shortly after, more shots rang out so close that Magnus could feel the concussion in his chest. Again, ringing assailed his ears, but he heard enough to recognize human voices, and that gave him hope. Something latched onto his clothes and pulled. He emerged from beneath one monster to face another: Lefty.

Magnus cleaned his face with a sleeve. "I fired a gun," he said, and was surprised by his own prideful lilt.

"I saw," Lefty replied. He pulled Magnus to his feet and waved off his attempt to return the revolver. "Hold onto it. No tellin how many we're up against."

"The wolf fell after I shot the center head."

Lefty considered this. "Three heads, one brain." He turned toward the other men and hollered, "Attack the center head!"

He stomped toward a group of wolves that were dragging a man along the ground. Magnus followed, his body vibrating with adrenaline. Sporadic gun blasts came from all directions, but he walked on without a flinch. When he caught up to Lefty, he saw that the man being dragged was Dingo. The jaws of the wolf at Dingo's head were latched onto a flap of skin from his skull. Lefty unslung his lever gun. He fired mid stride at the beast's center head and felled it. He worked the lever and fired again and again, each bullet destined for its own mutated wolf.

Magnus slowed, allowing Lefty to eliminate the threats before he continued toward Dingo. He had to admit, Lefty's killer competence was impressive—inspirational even. He emptied the lever gun then crouched and laid it across his thighs. Reloading with one hand, he wielded his second revolver with the other, and when the operation was complete he brandished the rifle once more, shooting with impeccable precision.

Lefty spun, lever gun pointed directly at Magnus, and fire exploded from its bore. A hiss and snap split the air so close to Magnus' face he could feel the rippling heat, but the only thing that rifled through him was an impulse to fire back. He aimed the revolver, but before he could pull the trigger the urge extinguished.

Lefty had already turned away. Of course he had. He would never have missed from this distance, not even in the dark. He had deliberately shot past Magnus. When Magnus looked, there was a wolf lying a few feet behind him, bloodied and twitching.

Magnus' next thought was of Stickman. If a trained killer like Dingo had gone down, what had become of the helpless young man. The worst seemed inevitable.

"Stickman!" Magnus called, his throat thick with worry.

Lefty whirled beside him. "Stickman!" It came out as a curse.

They continued to call for him, and Magnus began to wander in concentric circles. He hadn't made it far before a body that he thought to be a corpse twitched in its supine position. Magnus stiffened. Swallowing a shot of fear, he inched closer. "Stickman, is that you?"

The corpse jolted again, and a bloody arm jutted out. A third arm. He could clearly see the original limbs still attached at the corpse's shoulders. Had it mutated—and so quickly? The third, smaller arm waved, and a muffled cry could be heard.

Magnus approached the dead man, a burly soldier

whose name he hadn't learned, and rolled him over. Stickman hinged up to a seated position, greedily sucking air.

Between gasps, he rambled in spurts too chaotic for Magnus to understand even if they were in English. Stickman's gaze found the gun in Magnus' hand, which hovered near eye level. Embarrassed, Magnus tucked the revolver into his waistband and proffered a helping hand. The young man's eyes traced the arm up to Magnus' face. He leapt to his feet and wrapped Magnus in a tight embrace.

"Thank you!" Stickman whispered into his ear.

He heard the words but was too overwhelmed by the sincerity of Stickman's embrace to respond. Had Magnus ever hugged anyone before? Surely he and Ingrid had, but there was a purity here, an unbridled vulnerability. Stickman's joy, loyalty, and trust permeated Magnus, warming him inside out. Beat after beat his heart absorbed the affection. He basked in it, and his chest swelled. Each contraction of that funny, fist-sized muscle grew softer, smoother, until its movement was liquid, its pulsing that of tiny waves against the sand. He was on a beach on the Gulf of Mexico, baked by the sun, soothed by the susurrus of rippling wake, caressed by the sea's saline currents. With a flare, his heart began to radiate a fondness of its own. He didn't wrap Stickman any tighter, merely tilted his head toward him, and that was the only signal Stickman needed to cinch down until Magnus' insides felt squished.

The moment shattered when a bullet smacked a nearby tree. Staying low, Magnus led Stickman by the hand back to Lefty. The captain nodded to Magnus, then stepped up and severed the grip he had on Stickman's hand. He guided the leash into Magnus' fingers then turned away without a word.

The night grew still as the remainder of the pack dispersed, running into the shadows. Lefty kneeled beside Dingo. Over his shoulder, Magnus could see that the lieutenant's throat was torn away.

Brown appeared at Magnus' side. "Shit, Dingo, god-damn dogs finally finished what they started."

Lefty spat. He reached for Dingo's gun belt and unbuckled it, slid it off the dead man, then stood and turned to Magnus. He extended both arms, the gun belt in his right hand and his left hand laid open, palm up. His fingers beckoned, and Magnus placed Lefty's revolver there. Without a word, Lefty dropped Dingo's belt into Magnus' empty hand.

Magnus stared at the leather band supporting two holsters. The weight of it surprised him. He couldn't imagine the discomfort of wearing it. "Oh, I don't…"

He looked up, to find that Lefty had already moved on and was speaking to Brown. "Kill the wounded. Cain't afford no deadweight with the rest of that pack still out there."

Wasn't *he* wounded? Magnus leaned for a view of Lefty's forearm, but his arms were crossed.

Lefty stepped forward to address the group. "Ain't no time for sentiment, boys. We gotta keep movin." When no protest was offered, he said, "After you, Mister Lief."

Magnus scanned the weary soldiers, his eyes returning to meet Lefty's impatient stare. "Right this way," Magnus said. Lefty had called him *mister* again. Had he earned the devil's respect? A part of him desired it second only to the pelts, a confusing revelation. He gestured toward the rocky slope rising before them. "Afraid that was the easy part, men. It's all uphill from here."

7

Two hours of marching passed without incident. Around them, pools of fog had condensed in ruts and shallow depressions, and the moon's emergence imbued them with silver iridescence. The foothills were a sea of fog. Only the tops of those unnaturally tall trees suggested that there was a planet below that inscrutable, swirling veil.

Their path grew steeper and rockier, at times forcing them to holster their weapons so they could use both hands to climb. Stickman managed these stretches tenuously, requiring considerable help from the other men. If the wounded had been dead weight, what did that make the frail, mostly blind young man? Worse yet, they were running out of time. The harbinger of dawn had arrived. The faintest glow was building in the east, only detectable against the horizon's silhouette.

"Step lively, men," Magnus said. "If we don't get there before dawn, the tedekar will go into hiding until nightfall."

The men grumbled, and Magnus dared not look back. They were losing faith. He didn't need to see their scowls to know their displeasure.

They arrived at the base of a crag spanning as far as they could see in both directions. It rose fifty feet before them, and while there had been no shortage of trees since they entered the forest, the sky above the rise was wholly unobstructed. Though Magnus had lost the trail long ago, the creatures they had encountered convinced him that they were on the right mountain.

A dissonant howl resounded from behind—far too close—and Magnus' gut wrenched. The wolves had followed, and they were up against a wall.

"I ain't lookin to be dog chow." Brown lifted one leg and plucked at the seat of his pants. "I's so nervous my asshole's gnawin my undies."

Another soldier asked, "Can't we go 'round?"

"There may not be a way around," Magnus warned.

"Ain't no time." Lefty looked up the crag. "We have to climb."

The soldiers climbed, each man for himself except for two on either side of Stickman directing his hands, and one climbing beneath to help with his footing. As he neared the top, Magnus heard scraping and shouting. He glanced just in time to see Stickman drop onto the man beneath, knocking him from the rock face. The men at Stickman's hands caught him, but the one beneath fell all the way to the slab below. Several three-headed wolves emerged from the shadows to inspect the hot meal.

Magnus clenched his jaw and completed the climb, and when he reached the top, he finally saw a familiar landmark: a serrated ridgeline and snow-capped peak in the shape of a tilted nightcap. His sight line was clear because the conifers that had once grown from the rise lay flattened. The expanse of level earth and uprooted trees stretched at least one thousand feet in all directions. To his left the sheer drop of the crag continued, curling around until it met a gradual slope at the far side of the landing. To his right was another smooth vertical rock face split by a great, yawning cleft. It was the type of cave that would attract wildlife. As big as it was, anything might lurk in its darkness.

He glanced at Lefty who was helping a soldier onto the landing, then whispered to the group, "Stay quiet and move for that slope."

None acknowledged the order, but all complied, weaving around upturned roots and over prostrate trunks. They made it nearly halfway before the soldier guiding Stickman lost his footing, cursed loudly, and tumbled over a trunk, yanking the young man down by the leash. Magnus froze and knelt. He scanned the men, all of whom had frozen and shrunk with him—praise their discipline. Their eyes were glued to the huge, dark cleft.

There was movement. Rocks clacked within, echoing out. Then came a long, vexed groan that rattled Magnus' ribs.

"Damn, Crow, told ya not to eat that fuzzy apple," Brown quipped.

Crow replied, "It was a damned peach."

"Nuh-uh. I knows a apple when I sees it, and that was a bad'n. Had more hair than my big toe."

So much for discipline.

"Quiet!" Lefty snapped as the face of a titanic bear took shape in the cleft.

Magnus' heart pounded double, blood vessels

engorging with every beat.

The creature emerged in the scant twilight, its steps marked by the rattle of a thousand bones. Its body glimmered with a million tiny lights. Was it covered in eyes? No, not eyes. Each strand of fur had grown thick and hard like a claw. Its entire body was covered with them and the moonlight glinted off the scale armor. The bear's face was lined with bony studs. They pushed through the flesh along its snout, across its cheekbones and brows, then retreated in rows to the back of its head.

It tramped toward them, stopped, and swayed curiously, testing the air.

"Ho-lee-shit," Brown whispered.

The bear stood on its hind legs and walked a few staggering steps. It towered several stories tall. Its massive arms extended outward, and the sound that followed was an avalanche of shale. There were two arms on each side of its body, though the lower set was not as robust as the upper.

Lefty whispered and aimed his lever gun but signaled for the men to hold fire. The beast batted at something in the air, something small. It was a dark bird of normal size, perhaps a chickadee or a warbler, and it zipped and swooped about the bear's head. The bear stepped forward, then back, teetering. The bird made another loop around the curious bear then flew off, buzzing low over Magnus' head on the way. *Buzzing.* It was a strange sound for a bird, but it quickly made sense when the hairy, segmented body and translucent wings he saw were not a bird's at all but a flying insect.

The bear lost its balance and staggered forward toward the hiding men. Its forepaws came down, their collision with the earth sending a tremor through Magnus. Dust rose and wafted slowly through their position.

Specks of dirt peppered Magnus' skin. He closed his eyes as they settled on his lids, lashes, cheeks, nostrils. Pressure built in his sinuses. There was a tightening within the bridge of his nose. He pinched it and held on. He couldn't sneeze. A sneeze would be the end of him and everyone else on this landing. After a few long seconds, the pressure relaxed.

Chu. Someone sneezed to Magnus' right.

The bear spun, unhinged its gaping maw, and unleashed a roar louder than ten train whistles and as deep as an earthquake. Magnus drew his revolver and propped his arms over the tree trunk. He aimed it at the bear. The soldiers opened fire; Magnus followed suit. Bullets struck the bear everywhere, but if any made it through, the bear showed no sign of injury. It didn't so much as flinch. All it did was charge.

"Spread out!" yelled Lefty.

Two men vaulted their cover straight into the bear's paws. Holding them on each side of its body, its upper and lower arms worked against each other, and the screaming men were torn apart. It tossed their remains, blasted another deafening roar, and rampaged around the landing.

Soldiers were pulverized beneath its paws as bullets warbled off its armor. The bear barreled straight at three men banging away with their impotent machines and swiped its claws through where they stood. The movement registered as a mere blur, but Magnus felt the rush of air and the dust it stirred. To his amazement, the men were still standing after the claws had raked through. *It missed*, he thought. But with a second glance, they had fallen into heaps.

Magnus hung his head and swallowed hard. He had emptied both revolvers' cylinders in a matter of seconds and had no idea how to reload the damned things. With a twinge of shame, he resigned himself to hiding as the rampage continued. Soldiers rushed the bear from all angles. One approaching from its backside launched himself against the hind legs. He managed to grip the claw-like growths and began climbing. Was the crazy bastard trying to mount the beast? The man hadn't even clambered to the top of the hind quarters when the bear turned and slammed its backside into the granite face.

The bear batted another rushing soldier. His body crunched like a pinecone underfoot. He soared through the air, off the crag, and into the forest below. The bear whirled, faced another approaching man. It lowered its head and roared directly at him. He stumbled to a stop then staggered aimlessly, bewildered. There was blood flowing from his eyes and ears. The miserable sight lasted several long seconds until the bear clamped its jaws over him.

Everything that moved died. Death swept Magnus up in a whirlwind of blood and bone and innards. There was no killing the titan. No one even bothered shooting anymore. This was the end of the line.

Magnus scanned the landing, wondering how many soldiers were left. A few men crouched behind fallen trees.

Others knelt behind boulders and laid low in the cratered earth. Brown was squatting in a tree throw. Lefty was in the next throw over. Magnus' jaw relaxed at the sight of the most savage man he had ever met. Relief? In all likelihood, Lefty would murder him before their quest was over, but to do that he'd have to kill the bear first. If anyone on earth could manage such a feat, it was the brutish captain. It allowed Magnus a spore of dingy, grubby hope, but a spore of hope was no small thing.

Beyond Brown and Lefty there was movement. A young soldier carrying a satchel sprinted across the flat toward Brown. Magnus recognized the satchel as the one Lefty had insisted they retrieve from the meadow. Cradling it in his arms, the boy slid into Brown's throw, but Brown's attention was on Lefty who was whispering and motioning emphatically. Brown nodded, flashed the mischievous grin of a child given permission to break the rules, and took the satchel from the boy.

He lifted the bag's leather flap. It was full of thin brown cylinders. In the dim light, they looked like wooden dowels. What in Sam Hill did they want with dowels? Brown glanced down at the satchel then looked up and spoke to Lefty. Among the string of words his lips formed was one that changed everything: *dynamite*. Brown unwound a fuse and shouldered the bag. He jammed a cigarette between his lips, struck a match, and lit it with surprisingly steady hands. He stood, crossed himself strangely—he dragged his finger up from his belly button to his lips where he licked it before twisting each of his nipples—and clambered out of the root hole.

"Hey, papa bear!" he screamed, but the bear didn't notice. He drew his revolver and emptied the cylinder at the titan. It still paid him no mind.

A groaning sound came from the cleft and *that* drew the beast's full attention. Just when it seemed things couldn't get any worse. Magnus' guts wrenched as the vibrations took full form in his ears. It was indeed the sound of another bear, no mistaking it, but despite its low-rolling timbre, it had the feeble, pleading lilt of a babe's mewl.

Brown's lips formed a devilish crescent. "Oh, you's a mama bear?" he asked as the bear started for the cave. His hand slipped into the satchel and withdrew a single stick of dynamite. He transferred the stick to his other hand and rummaged again, emerging with a scrap of fuse maybe a foot long. He inserted the fuse and held the loose end to the cigarette's tip as he puffed it to a fiery glow. The cord began to hiss and spark, and the bear's movement came to a halt. It stood, twisted, fixated on the strange, glittering sight.

Brown waved the lit stick of dynamite in his left hand. The bear's mesmerized gaze followed its movement. He held the satchel's long fuse to the sparks, and it too flickered alight. Shrugging the satchel from his shoulder, he held it like a sling and took measured steps toward the mouth of the cave as the sparkling starburst held the monster's attention. Bit by bit the fuses burned shorter, the seconds ticking away. Brown needed to get rid of the damn thing before he blew himself and the rest of their dynamite to smithereens.

Just when Magnus drew breath to say as much, Brown

yelled, "I got yer porridge—extreee hot!"

He lobbed the single stick toward the bear's face, then darted into the cave. Magnus made out the word "Browndilocks" before the dynamite detonated against the bear's swatting paw.

The concussion bludgeoned Magnus' ears, and a laggard reflex bid his hands to cover them. His eyelids clamped shut as a corridor of pain connected between his ears. He forced his eyes back open and, through shimmering tears, observed the bear disappearing into the cave after Brown, its roars doubly vicious. Manic. Primal.

An eerie silence fell. The satchel of dynamite hadn't detonated. Would it? There was no way of knowing how long the fuse would take, but it seemed most probable that it was never going to explode, that it had been snuffed out or knocked free, and that they were out of options.

They did have one thing going for them. The bear was back in the cave, and that gave them an opportunity to move. Just then Lefty arose, signaled, and the remnant followed him in creeping along the landing.

Magnus had taken less than twenty steps when a sound from the cave brought the giant bear's face into view once more. Its lip was raised in a snarl and thunder issued from its throat. Was it staring at…him? His heart leapt in terror. His muscles twitched with false starts. He had to run; *they* had to run. It was their only chance. Why did it have to be this difficult? He wanted to collapse, to give up on the pelts, to melt into the earth and exist no more.

But for all their woes, the bear wasn't attacking yet. It had caught them all out in the open, and it hadn't even emerged from the cave. It just stood there, guarding the mouth with a threatening snarl.

It was then that the satchel detonated.

A geyser of blood and stone erupted from the cleft. The earth convulsed and the ground fell away from Magnus' feet. The shock hammered the air from his lungs. Breathless and unmoored, he tumbled rearward.

Magnus somersaulted and slid to a stop. Red rain began to sprinkle down, and the earth groaned. He dragged himself around to witness the cave's collapse. Relief oozed through him, but there was no time to relax. The sun was on its way. Against the aching in his body, he fought to his feet.

Stickman! How could he have gone so long without thinking of his young friend? Was he hurt? Magnus called out, but the atmosphere only rang a shrill reply. Even his own voice was little more than an undulating hum. Wheeling around, he staggered this way and that. After a minute he discovered the overall-clad native laying with his head against a bloodied rock.

"No, not Stickman," Magnus pleaded, a stone forming in his throat.

He rushed to the young man's side, knelt, and carefully tilted his head for a better look. The blood undoubtedly belonged to Stickman. There was a split four inches long in the back of his scalp that would need stitching, and any impact strong enough to cause such a laceration could have cracked his skull. There was too much blood to tell.

Placing his ear over Stickman's nose, his cheek over the boy's mouth, Magnus listened for breath while watching his chest. Warmth puffed against his cheek, and he heard no wheezing or hitching. Magnus sat back on his heels and turned his attention to Stickman's abdomen. That's when the boy gasped, yelled something unintelligible, and sprung to a seated position with arms braced behind him.

Magnus squatted beside Stickman and placed an arm around his shoulders. "I'm here, friend. Go slowly. Just breathe."

The young man reached a hand to the back of his head, winced when he felt the wound, and began to cry. He couldn't allow Stickman to cry in front of soldiers who measured men by their scars, scalps, and kills. Shushing him, Magnus scanned the landing for other survivors. They stood like petrified ghouls, more than a dozen of them, covered in dirt and blood.

"That's enough, Stickman," Magnus said. He stood and extended a hand.

Stickman wiped his mud-streaked cheeks against his shoulders, grasped Magnus hand, and struggled to his feet.

"We need to put some distance between us and this tomb," Magnus announced to men with wooden faces. "Who knows what that explosion will attract."

They started forward, Magnus leading Stickman by the hand, when Lefty eclipsed them. He snatched the young man's leash and gestured for Magnus to move ahead. Stickman wilted before Magnus' eyes. His shoulders slumped, spine hunched, head hung, and his strides flagged to a reluctant shuffle.

Curse that thin leather strap, and curse the hands that held it.

Magnus' blood writhed with ire. An impulse shot through him, and he winced. When he opened his eyes, the leash was in his hand. Lefty whirled around, teeth bared. Their eyes met, and despite Lefty's naked rage, Magnus held his gaze. His muscles trembled with adrenaline. He drew Bull's knife. Lefty's hand dropped to his revolver grip. Eyes locked on the captain's, Magnus began carefully cutting the collar from Stickman's neck. Lefty took a step toward him, but Magnus raised the knife in his direction.

"Stay back."

"Strap's for his own good, ya fool. How else ya gonna lead him?"

"By the hand, like a human being."

Magnus finished with the collar, then doubled the leash several times, folded it over the blade, and sawed through it. It fell to the ground in pieces. He sheathed the knife, took the young man's hand, and marched past Lefty.

Lefty didn't draw his gun, but the malice in his eyes made it clear that a bullet was on its way. Not just *a* bullet, *the* bullet. The one that had been destined for his skull from the moment he stepped inside the Withered Lizard. Had this been a huge mistake? Had there been another way?

Magnus pondered this as he led Stickman across the landing. After cresting the ridge, they descended through a crevice and negotiated a copse of large blue spruce. Ten minutes later they emerged, standing before a scenic lake within a massive crater. His crater.

Magnus stopped the men and said, "This is where the herd crosses." His gaze swept through the tangerine sky. "They'll be here soon."

The weary soldiers plopped onto logs and rocks, most of them bleeding, all of them panting from the thin atmosphere. Magnus reached into his vest and withdrew the small bottle of whiskey he had purchased from the hotel bar.

He cleared his throat. "I was saving this for a toast, but that hardly seems appropriate now, so…let's just call it medicine."

He removed the cork, passed it around, and every man took a stiff pull except for Stickman, whom he skipped. Instead, as the other men were distracted, he squeezed his right index fingertip harder and harder until the skin began to darken. Black liquid leached through the pores and beaded like sweat. The beads swelled and merged into a single orb the size of a pea. After a few seconds the orb coagulated. Magnus rolled it between his thumb and index finger. He opened his hand and the tiny black marble rolled down the crease between his fingers and into his palm.

"Here, Stickman, eat this," he said.

Without question, Stickman popped it in his mouth.

Magnus sat on a log, wiped his brow with his crusty sleeve, and beheld the serene turquoise depths that had not existed when last he was there. He had made it. Against abysmal odds, unnatural horrors, and treacherous company, he had returned before time expired. Closing his eyes, he retreated into himself and partook in a rollicking, triumphant jubilee.

By the time he finished the celebration and opened his eyes, Lefty and his soldiers were unconscious.

8

Lefty emerged from oblivion. He strained to open leaden eyelids, but they withstood his exertions. Hell of a strange sleep it had been, more like being buried alive. The world went black, and a cold, smothering weight pressed down on him so that he couldn't move or hear or even think. But there *had* been thoughts. In fact, he had figured something out in that absolute darkness. What had it been? The taste of stale, sweet campfire came in his reverie. The campfire in the meadow? No. It was there, on his tongue, tingling. Whiskey.

Lief!

The goddamned coward had poisoned the coffin varnish! If he could move any part of his body, starting with his fucking eyelids, he'd strangle the lickspittle and savor every kick, wriggle, and spasm until his chest quit rising. "Why can't I see?" he screamed, but the words resonated dully inside his head.

A fever of fury consumed him, but even it failed to melt the bitter cube of cold, hard regret nesting heavily in his gut. Lefty's instincts had been true after all—of course they had. He never should've left the Withered Lizard. He never should've given up scalping contracts, assassinations, and hunting bounties. He had been untouchable. He had been a god. He had it all until Magnus Lief waddled into their lives too rich and too stupid to resist.

And yet, here they were. The pompous, pious, perfidious Magnus Lief had bested him.

How had things gone so wrong?

Listless, Lefty quit all hope of opening his eyes, and it was then that the darkness gave way to a sky alight with powdery shades of orange and lavender. He attempted to sit up but felt untethered from his body, as if all that was left of him was a face and the brain behind it. Was he breathing? Yes, the nip of cold mountain air in his nostrils told him that.

A familiar voice sharpened into focus, and he felt his jaw inching forward with each word, teeth grinding like worn gears.

"When this is over, will you come with us?" Magnus Lief asked.

Lefty rolled his head, surprised by his neck's obedience, and saw Lief holding a ledger. Free of his collar, Stickman stood beside him goggling it with crisp brown eyes.

Again, Lefty tried to speak. "Your eyes…"

Stickman's head yanked up at the weak croak. He was smiling. It was an awkward, unflattering expression that Lefty would not have forgotten had he seen it before. "My friend fixed them!"

Lefty snorted, attempting to glare. "How nice. By what sort of black magic did he manage that, I wonder?"

Stickman frowned, "No magi—"

"I taught ya better than to trust men like Lief." Finally his voice came out strong.

"*You* follow him here," Stickman said, his brow raised in an accusing arch. The little shit.

"I believe he meant to take advantage of me," Lief remarked.

"Damn right I did, but I didn't know what you were then."

Lief stroked his chin. "Do you now?"

"Show him," Stickman prodded, pointing at the lake. "Show him!" His smile was broad and dirty. Lefty had never seen him so excited.

"Alright, alright. As you wish, my friend." Lief hooted and patted Stickman on the shoulder. "He really has rallied since I removed that dreadful collar and repaired his eyes. Amazing what happens when you care for the people around you rather than kill them." Lief ran his finger along something in his palm and a black object with a pitted surface like lava rock materialized out of a shimmering vail in the center of the lake. It would be the biggest ship Lefty had ever seen if it were a ship. But despite its position in the lake and its vaguely nautical shape, he was rather certain it wasn't meant for water. The fool shuddered with excitement.

"Looks like a black turd," Lefty croaked.

"It doesn't look like much, I know, but nothing gets a load of cargo out of an atmosphere more efficiently." Lief chortled triumphantly.

"Atmosphere? Ya mean…" Lefty rolled his eyes sky-ward.

"Yes, it flies. Well, it used to fly. Someday your kind will probably call it a sky carriage or a star wagon or something equally mundane." Lief harrumphed.

"My kind?" Lefty considered the implications. Lief waited, looming in a way that reminded Lefty of his childhood teacher. Fuckin math. He took a stab. "You ain't human."

Lief's pink mouth formed a grin.

"Of course you're not. I assume that's your nightmare zoo back there."

Magnus' face screwed in puzzlement. "Oh, no. We didn't bring those beasts with us. I fear we are responsible for their creation, though. The ship's power core was damaged in the crash. I believe it's been leaking quasnine into the lake. Everything drinking from it and its runoff has mutated. According to our scans, Earth doesn't have quasnine. I think it's safe to say your ecology is incompatible."

"Ya don't say." Lefty huffed a silent laugh. He wasn't sure what else to do. This was the most cockamamie bullshit he'd ever heard, but he couldn't dispute any of it. The last twelve hours was all the impossible proof he needed. "This changes nothin."

Lief's smile grew. He cocked an eyebrow. "Is that so?"

"It is. This is all gonna end the way it always was. It's your destiny. Don't matter what you are or where you're from."

"I suppose happily ever after is out of the quest—"

"I'm gonna put a bullet in your fuckin head." Lefty tried to laugh but emitted only a strained wheeze. A flapping wheel spun between his lungs provoking a violent coughing fit. The convulsions eventually settled and, lungs burning, Lefty's gaze again found Lief's. A mist of spittle fell to his cheeks and forehead.

Lief ignored the threat, turning toward his partly submerged ship. "We made the crater when we crashed. I should've anticipated the lake; it's been five years. Our first thought was to repair the ship, but Earth doesn't have the materials for our power cells." Lief paused, holding eye contact with Lefty. The round fool's eyes were darker than he remembered—reflective—and as he spoke, they became solemn. He frowned and shook his head. "We deviated from our programmed course. None of my people even know we're here. At least, I can't imagine how they would."

"I don't give a damn."

Lief's mouth flattened at the dismissal. "I'll never understand you, Captain. Despite your attempts to disguise it, you're obviously an educated man and, clearly—" he gestured to the unconscious soldiers on the ground beside Lefty "—a natural leader, for better or worse."

"Leave them outta this. They just followed orders."

Lief's brow furrowed. He blinked and shook his head. "You're missing the point. You have no vision. Your intelligence is squandered on small thinking. You interact with a being from another planet, likely one of the first humans to ever knowingly do so, and all you want to do is kill it."

Oh, he would kill it alright, and soon. He didn't need to fully regain his strength; all he needed was a working trigger finger to bring this infestation to an end, and he'd have that lickity split. The numbness was fading. His stomach had gurgled, and he had felt every puckered flatulence. A thousand scurrying rodents had been traveling through his arms and legs for minutes now. It wouldn't be long until his muscles would respond to commands.

Lefty replied, "You're leavin out the part where you led us to the slaughter, an' something tells me you ain't done yet. I've killed for less."

"I've watched you do it."

"Magnus"—his tongue prickled bitterly with the word—"ain't even your real name is it?"

"No, but it may as well be." Lief sighed. "It's what you bipedal barbarians will be calling me for the next thousand Earth years, or whenever your kind's technology advances enough to get us off this rock."

"I really doubt ya got that kind of time."

Lief huffed. "You're probably right. We do have to make it back down off this mountain, after all."

"If 'we' is just the two of you," Lefty said, flicking his eyes between Lief and Stickman, "you might as well kill yourselves now. Make it quick an' painless."

"Oh, there *are* more of us. In fact, there are more than the twelve we started our mission with. I was the first officer. Nine died during the crash, a tenth shortly after, but I survived along with an engineer—my dear friend. We'll just call her Ingrid."

"Where's she?" Lefty asked. He didn't give a shit, but it bought him more time to recover. "Ya get her killed too?"

Lief sighed deeply. "I suppose I did. She was killed when we first attempted to traverse that forest." Lief flicked his soft chin in the direction from which they had come.

"That's how ya knew you needed soldiers." A low chuckle rose up within Lefty's chest. He fought it and lost. His body convulsed and a grating pain rippled within his torso. Pain. Sensation. Control would come soon. He need only delay a little longer.

What a one-legged hoedown this had been.

"So why the hell we even here?" Lefty growled. "You were clearly tellin' a thumper 'bout the tedekar—" Lefty grimaced as his intestines shifted.

"Well—"

"Shut yer trap!" Blood surged through Lefty's neck, swirled in his ears. "It don't matter why. I'm gonna kill ya. I'll kill ya, slap ya awake, an' kill ya again! I'll kill ya fifty times over before I'm finished!"

Lief stiffened. His face crinkled. "And how, exactly, will you accomplish that, Captain?"

"You're fixin to find out—"

Sharp pains flared in Lefty's groin and corkscrewed down the inner flanks of his legs until they reached his toes. Fire twirled beneath his toenails, searing as if they were being torn away. He growled in agony, a growl that softened to a howl, and eventually a hoot. By the end he was laughing. It was the first time he had felt anything below the nuts and, unpleasant though it was, he was glad to have it back.

Lefty opened his eyes to find Lief gawking. "That seemed unpleasant!" He slapped his knee and looked at Stickman who was also starting to laugh, albeit with a measure of uncertainty.

"Don't you dare, Stickman!" Lefty snapped.

Stickman's laughter faltered. He glanced from Lief to Lefty.

"Don't you dare side with him. You're gonna let him kill me an' the men? He ain't even human. What kind of person betrays his fellow man?"

"You." Stickman crossed his scrawny arms.

That little traitor was lost. "If that's how it is, Stickman, you deserve what's comin' as much as him."

The boy broke eye contact with Lefty. His gaze wandered in worried thought.

Magnus intervened before Stickman could waver. "Tough talk, Captain, but the cards are down and you've lost."

Lefty's cheek twitched. He forced words between his teeth. "Oh, I got an ace up my sleeve yet…"

"An ace?" Lief chortled. "It wouldn't matter if you had a genie up there. I'm afraid the machinations of your demise have been set in motion." Lief's expression went completely blank. His eyes rolled upward until only white remained. A series of bizarre tones, pulsing and melodic like a singing telegraph, emanated from Magnus' abdomen. The notes shifted, passing through frequencies that tingled, and trembled, and hammered, and resonated.

Then, at once, the tones ceased.

Movement at Lefty's right caught his attention and he turned. His soldiers laid there along the shore, torsos bulging and rolling like sacks full of chickens. Their bodies spasmed in rhythm. The churning quickened to a flutter. For what felt like minutes, Lefty watched his men convulse on the rocky shore, unnerved by the thump of boots and heads against stone, the rustle of fabric in flux, the murmur of air expelled through slack lips. Eventually, the men stilled, but the calm was short-lived. His soldiers bolted upright and wavered gently—awoken from a terrible sleep. Their jaws dangled and their eyes jittered as though reading at blistering speeds.

Lefty's jaw clenched tightly, driving nails of pain through his teeth and into jawbone. The muscles of his face knotted with uncontrollable fury. He yelled through constricted lips, "Fuck you! You cain't kill my men like this!" He strained for command of his unresponsive arm and managed only twitching fingers. "I cain't even move, ya meater! I shoulda killed ya the moment your lard ass walked into the saloon!" Pressure built behind Lefty's eyes and the treetops that bordered his vision began to whirl. His brain did a somersault inside his skull, and something hot climbed up his esophagus. Black dots multiplied in his vision.

Lief shouted over the commotion. "The hatchlings inside your men are eviscerating many of the organs in their abdominal cavities. Certain vital tissues will be spared, principally the brain, as it facilitates bodily control and social integration. It's beneficial to know everything that the host knew."

One word Lief said stood out to Lefty. "Hatchlings?"

"That's right and, to answer your question, that's why we're here. As I said, the ship's power core was damaged upon impact. Life support's been running on reserve to keep the hatchlings alive and sedated. We calculated it would last five years, and five years it's been. If I didn't get you here soon the hatchlings might've perished, my mission failed."

Clarity's clammy palm finally slapped sense into Lefty. His epiphany was birthed in a foul utterance. "Shit, we're the fuckin pelts."

Lief confirmed this with a single nod.

"I ain't goin out like that." The words didn't come out as powerfully as Lefty felt them. Bubbles danced around his abdomen and down his legs. They induced tension there, a tension that felt a lot like strength. He commanded his leg muscles to flex, and they obeyed, albeit reluctantly. He tried his trigger finger again, and this time it curled until the nail dug into the meat of his thumb. In a minute he would take matters into his own hands.

"No? Well, Captain, today's your lucky day." Lief crouched and gestured toward the soldiers. "My species can manipulate the directives of the human body. We can sustain it, control it, and repair it as I have done with Stickman's eyes." Lief propped a hand on the toe of Lefty's boot. "But you will not become a pelt. You will endure a more fitting destruction." He stifled a snicker.

"Lucky me," Lefty said, shrugging—*actually* shrugging.

Lief didn't seem to notice the movement, nor did Stickman. In fact, Stickman wasn't looking at Lefty at all. His sharp gaze was trained slantways on Lief, and his hands wrung the binding of the innkeeper's ledger.

Ever oblivious, Lief just kept talking.

"There is a small sphere of quasnine inside of your body, implanted while you slept. Day by day its radiation will alter your outward appearance to match the monster within." He held as if expecting applause. "Oh, come on. You have to admit it's rather poetic, Captain."

"Never had much use for poetry."

Lefty's intestines wriggled. His abdomen bulged until the fabric of his uniform bound its progress. Lief stepped back as pain slashed across the bloated flesh. Surely he was about to split wide open. He watched in horror, expecting the blue wool to darken with wet stripes and his entrails to rise through the fissures like charmed snakes. The deformation came to an abrupt end just as a coat button popped free. Save the rise and fall of his frantic, shallow breaths, Lefty's torso settled. He trained his blurred vision on Lief once more.

The extraterrestrial shook his head in disbelief. "Pickle my peppers, I *am* amazed. It's happening even faster than I had expected. Almost too fast. Can't have him chasing us back down the mountain, can we, Stickman?"

Stickman wagged his head.

Lefty's jaw muscles strained against the enamel within. Teeth. Gnashing, gnawing, rending teeth, that's what Lief deserved. He wanted to bite, to chew, to crush the man into pulp, bit by bit.

Except he wasn't a man, was he? As far as Lefty knew, the creature inside Lief was already pulp—nothing to bite, nothing to chew, just tar or some other black ooze that would slip between his teeth, slide down his throat, and choke him out.

What a bad box this he was in, but he wasn't defeated yet. That was the thing about bad boxes, there was always a way out. This would be no different. After all, he did still have an ace. A way to prove himself right. A way to smite.

"Shall we tie him to a tree?" Lief asked before answering himself. "Yes, I think we shall."

When Lief stooped to gather a rope, Lefty recognized the only opportunity he was likely to get. With mortal urgency Lefty demanded action, and his body finally delivered. He slipped his left hand into his right sleeve, grabbing the stubby grip of his Remington Model 95 Derringer.

"Lief, you're the worst kind of monster: the kind that don't know he is one. Since your cards are down, here's mine: an ace of spades, just for you."

Before Lief could utter a sound, Lefty slid the Derringer from its holster, aimed, and pulled the trigger. His trusty barking iron released a bloodthirsty roar. Lief's head bulged and withered in an instant, its contents floating off in a pink cloud.

"Magnus!" cried Stickman as Lief collapsed.

Lefty cocked the hammer and spun the Derringer toward the boy lunging for Lief. Stickman stiffened.

"Eh, eh, eh, boy. Stay back. Your *friend's* gonna need a new pelt. Since mine's contaminated, that leaves you." He snickered. "Thankfully, I know the only thing ya really care 'bout in this life: your sister. Itamah, right? It's been a few years an' a lotta scalps, but I do recall sellin her to a slaver outta Arkansas—Rinkleman was his name." Pain swelled beneath his sternum and he gasped. Panting, he continued, "Odd name, Rinkleman, but fortunate. Wouldn't of remembered it otherwise. Doubtful your sister's still there, but it's a start. I thought ya might need a reason to fight, an' now ya have it. Kill that thing inside Magnus before it kills you, an' go get your sister. Be a man for once in your pitiful life."

Lefty winked at Stickman, jammed the warm muzzle against his own temple and fired his final bullet

9

Tears stung Stickman's eyes, but he fought the urge to blink. The pain brought relief, though not nearly enough. A shimmering veil coated his eyes until the world around him appeared submerged, washed clean by his sorrow. When he finally blinked, his eyelids loosed the torrent down his cheeks, over his lips, and onto his awaiting tongue. *Disgusting saltiness.*

As his vision cleared, he found that the carnage remained. It was inescapable. The captain's brains were only the latest brushstroke in a masterwork of horror. At the Captain's feet lay Magnus, his hollow head flattened like an empty water skin.

Remembering the soldiers-turned-pelts, Stickman spun to find them still sitting on the shore in a tidy row, blankly staring across the crater lake. What now? What would those beings do when they took full control of their pelts only to find Magnus dead or, if the captain was right, in desperate need of a new pelt? Would the creature inside Magnus remember their friendship? Stickman didn't want to find out.

He gathered from their meager reserves a half-empty canteen, two handfuls of jerky, a pouch of nuts, a bedroll, a hatchet, a coat, and a wide-brimmed straw hat which, paired with the overalls, made him look like a farm boy. The supplies weren't enough, but they fit in one of the soldier's satchels and carrying more would only slow him down. He couldn't risk being in the forest after dark.

With a stride toward the copse of blue spruce, Stickman spared a final glance at Magnus Lief, guilt twisting his guts. Magnus had healed his eyes, removed his collar, and saved his life. They had bonded over art, and Magnus had never made him feel worthless or ashamed. Now Magnus was laying there with a collapsed head and slashed belly. Stickman took a second step before the observation registered.

Magnus' belly was split open. It wasn't split before.

Stickman turned to leave just as an oily silhouette arose a few steps ahead. It assumed the familiar height of Magnus Lief in bipedal form. Stickman's head bobbed with his pulse and his ears rang with pressure. He dropped a trembling hand to the knife belted around his waist and drew it, aiming the unsteady point at the creature.

"Stickman." The word formed from vibrations all over the figure's corded flesh. It stepped closer.

"Magnus?" Stickman's eyes flicked to his friend's hollow corpse. There was no such person. He backpedaled with the knife outstretched.

The creature raised black hands that had the look of bundled twigs. "It's okay, Stickman. I won't hurt you."

Stickman hesitated, shoulders rising and falling with shallow breaths. "No. You need a pelt."

"Yes, but not yours. Never yours, my friend." There was warmth in the words. "Just put the knife away so we can figure this out." Stickman's neck hair prickled. "Lefty really left us in a predicament. But—"

If Stickman were to close his eyes, he would never know he spoke with a being from another world. Only the way that the sound entered his ears so indirectly hinted that something was strange about old Magnus Lief, but it *was* Magnus' voice. It sounded exactly the same, and it was hard to ignore that familiarity despite the form of black and twisted lines he saw.

Stickman's tension melted.

Magnus was still talking. "We already needed more pelts as it was. The hatchlings doubled inside those soldiers won't share for long."

Stickman nodded, but pressure was building between his eyes. *More* pelts? It wasn't over. He had no love for Lefty's men, but it was horrible watching their guts churn and it was awful to think that they might still be alive in some way, trapped in bodies that would never die. No one should suffer that, and Magnus needed *more* pelts. It was all so tiring. "I do not want more people to die."

Magnus stepped closer and spoke softly. The vibrations now came from the area of a human mouth. "I don't either, but I have no choice. We can't survive your sun's rays without pelts."

Stickman was stuck.

Magnus had every right to protect himself and the hatchlings, but "protection" meant death, and Stickman had seen too much of that already. He didn't want anyone else to die, but his wants had never meant anything to anyone. How stupid had he been to think he was free? Free of Lefty, maybe, but Lefty had only been the servant of a greater power, an evil that yanked all creatures by an invisible leash. That was why the choice was not *if* someone would die but *who* would die. How maddening!

Frustration spilled from Stickman's eyes, and his lungs began to quiver, but it wasn't just his emotions that left him short of breath. Magnus wrapped himself around Stickman's shoulders. A hug? It was awfully firm but still gentle, and with his eyes closed he could mostly forget the fact that his comforter was a shifting mass of cords and strands.

Lefty was wrong; Magnus was a true friend.

The hug tightened, and Stickman released all stress. Nothing had been resolved, but that warm embrace assured him that all would be okay.

"Thank y-you." Stickman's voice hitched as his sobbing slowed.

"I've upset you. The least I can do is offer my shoulder."

A second set of limbs slinked around Stickman's ribcage. A third around his hips. He was a child again, swaddled tightly in his cradleboard. Secure. Safe. Strength rippled through the cords of tissue, and Stickman felt as though he were buried among the roots of a great oak tree. No one had ever hugged him that way, especially not while he was crying. His own father had turned away at such emotion. He had always felt things more strongly than others. It was no choice of his own, but it shamed him anyway.

As unlikely as it was, he took comfort in the idea that

he was normal and everyone else was missing a piece of their humanity. The longer he lived, the more people he met, the easier it was to believe that.

Stickman began to warm from the outside in. The first touch of glorious heat raised waves of goose flesh. It worked through him, thinning his blood and kneading his muscles. After the chaos of the last several months, he thought such peace was impossible.

Stickman opened his eyes to blinding sunlight, and to an oily writhing creature.

Magnus' human features dissolved as his form shifted and bulged. He was fraying. Strands of that braided flesh snapped and peeled back, twitching like spider legs. One gave way near Stickman's cheek with a soft hum and rattle. Its sound met that of a dozen others to create a sizzle that Stickman could not only hear but *feel*. His arms, still wrapped around what had been Magnus' torso, tingled with the release of thread after thread.

He pushed back and tried to wiggle free. Magnus' limbs squeezed tighter still. Stickman squirmed for escape as Magnus' wooly flesh drew nearer. Tattered fibers caressed his cheek and tickled his neck as Magnus' form pressed into him. Stickman turned to the sky for breath. His eyes closed as his mouth opened for a gulp. Air filled his lungs…and then stopped. Something other than air was pouring in, braided and rough, like an old rope. He gagged as the frayed tentacles of Magnus flesh plunged into his throat.

A white and ravenous fire sparked inside Stickman's chest. Its heat took control, and he found himself flailing.

Flailing? *His arms were free.* The realization brought hope, but that hope demanded violence. Blow after blow his knuckles rapped against Magnus' flesh, panic snapping through his muscles. He tried to cry out, to scream for the shadows, to beg the soldiers to stop Magnus, but his voice was gone and the words burned desperately in his lungs.

Stickman's head grew light and the burning in his lungs spread into his muscles. A torrid wave passed through him, and, in its wake, a terrifying numbness such that he wished the burning would return. He swung his right hand with every bit of strength he could, praying it would be enough but knowing it wouldn't. This was death, killed by the monster inside his friend. He swung again, weaker still.

Magnus spasmed with the hand's impact.

Stickman felt the tentacle jolt all the way down his throat, deep into his guts. Something about that blow was different. It got Magnus' attention. So, Stickman did it again. And again. There was no thought in it. His body became an engine of violent action lashing out at the creature that brought pain.

Each swing of Stickman's scrawny arm drove Magnus back more. It was working! Hope sprouted and ripened all at once. Stickman jabbed even harder until Magnus' weight finally fell away, and only then did he remember the tentacle running through his innards. A bolt of lightning exploded up his torso, toad to teeth.

What followed was an empty ache so deep that he knew it would never leave him. Had the vine split him in half? He lowered his gaze to discover blood glistening over every inch of him from the chest down. He stood in a pool of it—still warm. It was his own. It had to be. But no, the blood he wore was mostly black. Magnus' then.

There was something in his right hand. Even before he glanced down, he knew what he would find—Bull's knife, dripping with Magnus' black-as-coal blood. Stickman dropped the disgusting weapon, fell to his knees, and vomited. What came up might as well have been a bucket of red-hot embers. The pain was enormous and blinding. A gasp drew the fire back inside. It swirled there, spreading through his lungs. He wretched again, and coughed, and noticed through tears that his vomit was bright red.

Doom rumbled in his loins. This wasn't just another wave, it was something more, something heavy. A ball of lead expanded inside of him, and the bigger it got the more it threatened to drag him down into the earth. And he *was* sinking…into the dirt…down into the cold and dark.

The last feeling that registered was…wood. He was made of wood. Like a stick. And a stick man was no man at all. So that's it. He was dead. Perhaps he always had been…

— ∴ —

Something cool caressed Stickman's cheek. He started, eyelids fluttering open. His breath rippled a red puddle on his right; a dozen blank faces looked down from his left. Soldiers. They loomed over him in expectation.

Something nudged his leg. Stickman rolled over, expecting the cannon ball in his gut to shift onto his spine, but it didn't. The heaviness that had been there before was completely gone. In fact, as he laid there staring up at the soldier-pelts, it seemed that he had never felt better. He sat up and wiped the caked blood from his cheek with a sleeve already blackened with organic crust.

A soldier reached a hand toward Stickman. The black-haired mule of a man had been, and he supposed still was, named Coal. What else would his name be? After all, Magnus had always just been the pelt's name.

Magnus.

Somehow, he had almost forgotten the traitor. The friend who had made him into a killer, who had done what Lefty never could. Suddenly, it occurred to Stickman that he wasn't actually sure he *had* killed Magnus. He had punched and stabbed until the monster fell away, but was it killed?

He twisted to find that the heap of black cord had become a pile of ash. Magnus Lief's withered skin laid beyond it. Soiled robes. He turned back to the sight of Coal's extended hand still hovering there.

Stickman grabbed Coal by the wrist and yanked himself up, all but toppling the soldier in the process. Their faces nearly collided, and Stickman held him there where the air reeked of iron and rot.

"You cannot have my pelt," Stickman said, his own voice muffled by the war drum in his chest.

Coal stole a glance past Stickman to Magnus' remains. "No problem, Sticky," came Coal's gravelly voice. "It's no good to us anyway." Coal raised two fingers to his eyes. "You're marked, amigo."

Stickman's eyelids fluttered over eyeballs that suddenly

felt too big. "Marked?"

"Mmhmm."

"What do you mean?"

"Hell, I dunno. I mean you're…off limits. It's like seein somethin you've never seen before and just knowin it ain't food."

"Marked by who? Magnus?"

Coal shrugged and cocked his head. "Who else?"

"No. He tried to kill me. I think he *did* kill me."

"I hate to break it to you, Sticky, but you ain't dead. So, if he did kill you, he didn't leave you that way."

"But…I killed him." Stickman's eyes welled with tears.

Coal put a hand on Stickman's shoulder and their eyes met. "Maybe, but the sun would've got him anyway, amigo."

Stickman's mind swirled with the horrible possibility that Magnus had never meant him harm. The notion threatened to rip him apart.

"Listen, Sticky. I've killed hundreds of men, but I still remember my first. It's supposed to feel shitty even when it needs doin. The best thing to do is move on to what needs doin next."

Stickman sorted his thoughts. "My sister."

"And before that?"

"The monsters."

Coal nodded. "One more thing…"

"Pelts."

"Mmhmm."

Stickman's gut churned at the thought, but with a glance back to the pile of ash that had been one of their kind outside of a pelt, he understood. He could at least protect the innocent from becoming pelts. "I choose who."

"Fair enough, Sticky." Coal snatched Stickman's hand and shook it. "Ready?"

"No," Stickman said, yanking his hand away. He stepped and stooped and scooped up Lefty's gun belt, holstering both revolvers. He glanced back at Coal and the other soldiers, none of whom seemed the slightest bit concerned that he had just armed himself. Stickman spun and scanned the ground until he found what he was after: the innkeeper's ledger. Tucking it under his arm, he knelt beside Magnus' pelt and arranged the empty flesh so that the face was staring back at him.

"You know, we really should leave so we can make it through the forest before dark."

"If you are scared, leave." Stickman plopped down beside the pelt, crossed his legs and opened the book to a blank page. Innkeeper's blunt pencil in his right hand, Stickman closed his eyes and reached out with his left. He touched the molted skin of a once-kind man. His fingers ran over wrinkles and ridges, hairs and pores, empty sockets and hollow features. Eyes shut, he felt them with one hand, and sketched them with the other.

When he finally finished, he set his gaze upon the ledger's yellowed paper and his hideously deformed portrait of a man. Whoever he had ended up drawing, it was just right.

He closed the book, stood, and faced the soldiers. "Now I'm ready."

ACKNOWLEDGMENTS

Pelts started small, but it was always destined for greater things. The characters couldn't be contained, much less explored, in the tight confines of a short story. Expanding a work can be tricky business, and I couldn't have crafted a story with such balance if not for the expert advice of dear friends and fellow writers, Darynda Jones, Caleb C.W., Corynn Tenny, and Tracie Campbell.

As always, my father, Gerry Mayes, read every iteration of this tale, providing valuable insights and keeping me sane when life tempted me toward crazed meanderings by moonlight. I am perpetually amazed by the seemingly limitless patience of my wife, Tanya, who has yet to demand I seek medical help for the computer growing out of my lap. Maybe she has a thing for cyborgs…that would explain it.

ABOUT THE AUTHOR

Phil Scott Mayes is the author of Verity Rising, A Sharpened Dagger, Pelts, and many more to come. An avid fan of horror and thriller genres, his works are grounded and gritty interpretations of supernatural, science fiction, and fantasy themes.

Born and raised in Michigan, he spent ten splendid years in New Mexico before returning to his home state with his wife and three children.

Scan the QR code for more from Phil Scott Mayes.

www.philscottmayes.com